IRON PRINCESS

Book Two of the Savage Trilogy

MEGHAN

NEW YORK TIMES BESTSELLING AUTHOR

MARCH

ISBN: 978-1943796120 7298 7885 9/18

Editor: Pam Berehulke
Bulletproof Editing
www.bulletproofediting.com

Cover design: @ Letitia Hassar
R.B.A. Designs
www.rbadesigns.com

Cover photo: Aleksandar Georgiev

Visit my website at www.meghanmarch.com.

ABOUT THIS BOOK

He's a mystery. An enigma.

His very identity is a secret buried beneath layers of deception.

He's also an addiction I can't shake. An attraction I can't fight.

And then I found out exactly who he is—a man more dangerous than the devil himself.

Now I need him in order to save everything that matters to me.

I have to pull back. Protect myself from the danger that haunts his every step.

Which would be easy . . . if I could stop myself from falling in love with him.

Iron Princess is the second book in the Savage Trilogy.

IRON
PRINCESS

CHAPTER 1

Present Day

"**A**SHES TO ASHES, DUST TO DUST, LOOKING for that blessed hope when the Lord himself shall descend from heaven . . ."

The priest murmurs the words I've heard too many times over a casket that shouldn't be here. None of us should be here. This funeral shouldn't even be happening.

As the priest continues to drone, I bow my head to stare at the blades of grass I've trampled into the dirt beneath my feet. I can't stand to look at that wooden box for another second.

I should be sweating in the heat under my layers of black, but the block of ice lodged in my chest keeps me frozen where I stand.

I don't feel the heat.

I don't feel anything.

I'm not sure I'll ever feel anything again.

I'm numb—except for the guilt.

I did this.

This is all my fault.

CHAPTER 2

Kane

Fifteen years earlier

THE BUS FROM THE AIRPORT WAS TAKING FOR frigging ever, but if I wanted to keep it a surprise, I couldn't call for a ride. I'd spent practically my last dollar to catch that flight, and my paycheck from Uncle Sam wasn't going to hit for a few more days. Not that it was much of a paycheck when you thought about what we went through.

That's what I signed on for in the army. *Honor. Country. Duty.* Those are things a man can believe in, along with surprising his mama with his unexpected leave.

The bus dropped us at the station, and I waited for two old ladies and another guy to get off before

I shouldered my duffel bag and climbed down the stairs. It was a mile to the house, but it was worth it. Ma would be surprised as hell.

I just didn't expect that I would be too.

Fifteen minutes later, I opened the back door and stuck my head inside the kitchen. Ma's old dog, Rudy, didn't bark to announce my arrival.

I crept inside and shut the door behind me, and finally heard rustling coming from the laundry room. Keeping my footsteps light, I moved across the polished wood floors down the back hallway as her blond head popped out of the room.

"Surprise!" I yelled, and she dropped the basket of clothes she was carrying and screamed, covering her mouth to cut it off before her gaze swung to mine.

"Ma! What the fuck happened? Are you okay?"

I kicked the laundry basket out of the way as I moved toward my mother. My mother with a fucking split lip and a bruise on her right cheekbone, despite her attempt to conceal it with makeup.

"Did you have an accident? What happened?"

"Kane, you didn't tell me you were coming home." Her voice held none of the excitement I thought it would.

I stepped forward and reached out to cradle her

face in my hands. "Ma, what the fuck happened?"

Her pale blue gaze, just like mine, dropped away. "Nothing. Just clumsy."

Chills rolled down my spine, and the hair on the back of my neck rose like a pissed-off dog's. There was only one explanation that made any sense, and it was the last one I wanted to hear.

I met her gaze for a beat. "Tell me he didn't do this."

Her gaze dropped to my chest. "Kane, don't go jumping to conclusions. It's not gonna do anyone any good. You know me. Clumsy old lady these days."

"You're not clumsy and you're not old. I'm gonna fucking kill that bastard for laying a hand on you." I released my light grip on her face to turn around. "He at work?"

Her attention cut to my face, her blue eyes wide with panic. "Please, Kane. You can't. Don't even think about it."

"Why not?" My hands shook with the rage charging through my bloodstream. "Court in session? Good. Then they can all watch me beat the judge to a pulp."

I took one step, but she reached out and grabbed my arm, her perfectly manicured nails digging into my skin.

"And what do you think is gonna happen when you leave? You think getting him all riled up is going to make it go better for me somehow?"

I turned, my jaw clenched. "Then I won't go back."

She gave my arm another tug. "You have to. You're making something of yourself. And if you don't, you'll go to prison. I'm not visiting my son in prison. You hear me?"

"Tell me this was the first time he's ever touched you." I knew no matter what she said, I wouldn't believe it, even though I wanted to. I hoped it would calm the storm raging in my blood.

The fine lines bracketing her mouth deepened into grooves as she pinched her lips tight. Her voice shook as she said, "It was my own fault. I dropped his favorite whiskey and the bottle shattered. He's just come off a terrible trial. I should've been more careful."

Listening to my mother try to justify my stepfather's actions was like someone taking a knife to my gut.

"Leave him, Ma. Now. Today."

Her lips trembled before they pressed together. "It's not a big deal, Kane. I swear. And I'm not gonna file for divorce over something trivial like this."

Trivial?

I shook my head as I listened to her. "How can you possibly think this is trivial? He fucking hit you. No man who raises a hand to a woman in anger can still call himself a man. He needs to be taught a lesson, and I'm sure as hell capable of being the one to teach it."

Her grip tightened. "Did you come back here to stir up trouble and make my life more difficult? Because that's what you're fixing to do. If you give a damn about my life and me living it as peacefully as possible, you'll pretend you didn't see a thing. I'll do a better job on my makeup after I fix up your room."

Disgust flooded my system, mixing with rage, and I didn't know what to do. I wouldn't be a man worth a damn if I let this go unpunished, but what kind of son would I be if I went against her wishes?

I pulled my arm free of her grip. "Don't bother fixing up my room. I won't stay here and face that bullshit excuse of a man without ripping the arms off his body and beating him to death with them."

The blood drained from her face. "Kane, please. Just . . . forget it all. You can't say anything to him. He's been under a lot of stress with this trial."

"Don't worry. I won't say shit to him, because he ain't gonna see me while I'm here. That man is dead to me."

"He's your stepfather."

"He's a fucking bastard. Has been since the day you married him."

"He took care of us when we needed it."

"Tell yourself whatever you want. I'll get you out of here, set you up near base, give you every dime of my paycheck, and make sure you don't want for anything. Just tell me you'll leave, and we'll pack the car right now. You'll be gone before he gets home for dinner."

"You know I'm not leaving your gran. She might not know my name, but I'm all she's got."

"Then we'll take her too."

Ma's eyes went hard, telling me I was wasting my breath. "You should go wash up for supper."

I squeezed my eyes shut and shook my head. "I'll find somewhere else to stay."

"Kane, wait—"

I turned and strode down the hallway.

⟡

With my duffel bag over my shoulder, I walked three miles to the only other place I could think to go. I pushed the front door open as chimes made out of spent brass jangled to announce my entrance.

"Be right with ya," a familiar gruff voice called from the back.

I breathed in the scent of gunpowder and mildew, and suddenly felt more at home than I had in that big, perfect house the judge had Ma spend all her time keeping fancy.

I crossed to the glass case holding shiny revolvers and matte-black pistols, letting my fingers trail across the top as I gazed down at the guns and wished I had one to go hunt down the judge and make Ma's choice for her.

Then again, she didn't want to visit me in prison.

"What can I help you with today, son?" The smoke-roughened voice came from the other side of the case, and I looked up. "Holy shit. Kane Savage. I had no idea you were home, soldier."

Jeremiah Prather, Bulletproof's proprietor, saluted me, and I returned the gesture.

"Surprise visit," I said. The forced smile that briefly curved my lips fell away just as quick.

His gaze drifted to where I was white-knuckling the bag over my shoulder. "Surprise for your ma or you?"

Something in his tone set me on edge. "The whole town know he's smacking her around?"

Jeremiah's expression turned rueful. "Gossips have just started catching on. Someone heard there was some kind of dustup over there the other night from a neighbor walking her dog, and speculation has been running rampant since your ma missed church but was spotted at the corner market in dark glasses and makeup caked on about an inch thick."

I swallowed the rage that threatened to choke me. "And no one did a damn thing?"

Jeremiah crossed his arms over his stout chest. "What do you expect them to do? Giles is in so deep with the chief of police and the DA, there's no one who would file a complaint if your ma had the willingness to try."

My stepfather, Bernard Giles, owned this town. Hell, the Giles family owned most of the parish. Anyone who pissed him off found themselves hauled in front of his bench before being dragged off in cuffs. His sentences were legendary for their lack of mercy, but no one dared speak out against him. Joining forces with his dirty brother of a DA and a crooked chief of police made them a lethal combination.

"I'm gonna kill him." There wasn't an ounce of hesitation in my tone, and Jeremiah had known me long enough to know I wasn't fucking around.

He glared at me, the lines in his leathery face

deepening. "Don't say that shit on camera, boy. You know better."

He retreated into the back office before reappearing a few minutes later. Instead of returning to his position in front of me, he went to the entrance, flipped the sign to CLOSED, and locked the door.

"Had to erase all the way to before you came in and turn 'em off. Last thing you want to do is give them the rope to hang you with."

I leaned back on the counter, my fists clenched at my sides. "Then give me a throwaway piece, and I'll be gone before they know I was here."

"Boy, I know you carry a gun every day for Uncle Sam, but what you're talking about is something totally different. You don't make a move like that without it staining you to the very core of your soul."

My teeth ground together. "You think I haven't already seen and done things that are gonna send me straight to the devil? Two tours in hell, and I didn't come back the same person I was when I left."

"I know. You don't have to tell me." Jeremiah raised his forearm, where the lines of his POW/MIA tattoo were blown out and fading. "But that's still different. Why don't you head out into the range and shoot a few boxes to take out some of that anger you got riding you. I'll grab you a gun. *My* gun."

His emphasis was no mistake, nor was his choice of weapon. Jeremiah knew, or at least he thought he knew, that I wouldn't use his gun to take out Giles. Wily old bastard.

He slipped out from behind the counter again and disappeared for a moment before coming back with an old .45. He laid it on the counter and grabbed three boxes of ammo from the shelf behind him. "If I don't hear you firing, I'll come track you down with my AK, and it won't be a good day."

I would have sworn nothing could have dragged even a hint of a genuine smile from me, but Jeremiah managed with his play on the lyrics of Ice Cube's *It Was a Good Day*.

"I'll be shooting, but when I'm done, I make no promises. I might even borrow that AK."

"Blow off some steam, get your head clear, and we'll talk some more. I ain't letting you do some fool thing without a fuck-ton of thought."

CHAPTER 3

Kane

I DESTROYED TARGET AFTER TARGET WITH THE .45, and with every shot, I pictured Giles's head. Instead of releasing and letting go, my anger flamed hotter than a forge and hardened into something honed and deadly.

Giles doesn't deserve to live. No man who raises his hand to a woman in anger does. The image of the makeup-covered bruise on my mama's cheek and her split lip was burned into my memory like a cattle brand.

If no one else in this town would take out the almighty judge from the all-powerful family, then I had no other choice I could live with. I'd disappear, go AWOL, maybe head down to Mexico and live on a beach for the rest of my days, drinking Corona and keeping tabs on Ma from long distance.

I pulled the trigger and the pistol clicked.

Empty.

I looked down at the box of ammo.

Empty.

That meant it was time.

I made my way down the hallway behind the empty lanes and back through the heavy metal door into the store, but Jeremiah wasn't alone.

I ducked my head, pulling my hat lower to conceal my identity from whoever was with him. The fewer witnesses, the better. "I'll get out of your way. I can take the back door out."

Before I could take two steps, the man standing at the counter in his slick suit turned to me.

"You're just in time, Savage."

Who the fuck is this guy? And how the hell does he know my name?

The back of my neck prickled with warning as I glanced up. "Don't think I know you."

His penetrating black stare didn't intimidate me, but it sure as fuck unsettled me.

"Name's Mount. I understand we have a mutual interest in Judge Giles."

I looked to Jeremiah with betrayal burning a hole in my gut. "What the fuck did you tell him?"

Jeremiah held up a hand. "Before you go tossing out threats or doing something rash, I called in someone who could help."

"Who? A hit man? Because I ain't got a dime to pay anyone, and I'd prefer to handle this on my own."

The man studied me closer. I wasn't sure what he was seeing, but I felt like he was drilling down to the very marrow of my bones.

"I don't do wet work anymore. Too many stained shirts. Pissed off my tailor."

"Then feel free to forget whatever Jeremiah told you, along with my name and Giles."

"Now, hold on, boy," Jeremiah said. "Mount's got a proposition for you. You might want to hear him out."

"I ain't your boy," I snapped.

"No, but your daddy and I served together, and I promised to watch over you. So get your ass in here and listen up. This kind of offer doesn't come around twice."

Jeremiah had never sold me out before, so this betrayal stung more than I expected, but I didn't have much of a choice. I shoved the empty .45 in the back of my jeans and let the range door close behind me.

"What kind of offer?"

Mount pulled a thick envelope from his pocket

MEGHAN MARCH

and dropped it on the counter. "Fifty grand. Half now, half when you finish the job."

My gaze cut from him to Jeremiah and back. "What the fuck are you talking about?"

He pushed the envelope toward me with a finger. "Twenty-five K. Half of your fee. You get the second half when Giles is dead."

What he was saying finally clicked. "You want to pay *me* to kill Giles? The man I already want dead? What the fuck kind of business is that?"

Mount's expression stayed stoic. "That's not all."

I crossed my arms over my chest. "Figured there was a catch. Might as well hit me with it."

Mount mimicked my posture, but for some reason, he looked menacing when he did. "After this is done, you do three more jobs for me. When those have been fulfilled, you can go on about your business."

"What the fuck kind of jobs? I'm not doing shit that I don't agree to first."

"Kills. Hits. Contracts."

"You want me to be your goddamned hit man? Because you don't do wet work anymore?" I jerked my gaze from him to Jeremiah. "Is this guy fucking serious? After the first one, I'll either end up in prison, the morgue, or in a third-world country."

Mount shook his head slowly. "No. Because first *you* have to die."

My mouth dropped open in shock. "The fuck did you say?"

"You take the twenty-five K and this phone." He pulled it out of his pocket and set it on the counter beside the envelope. "We arrange to fake your death—throw your dog tags on a body, shove it in a shit car, burn it. Then we change how you look so not even your own mother would recognize you. Last, I tell you when and where, and you take out Giles. Call when the job's done and you get another twenty-five K. After that, you answer when I call, do the three jobs for the same price, and then you can decide where the hell you go from there."

I swallowed. Jesus fucking Christ. He had it all figured out, and I was still struggling to believe we were having this conversation to begin with.

"You're serious?" I asked. "You want me to . . ." I replayed it all in my head again.

"Yes. You have five minutes to decide before I walk out that door and my offer disappears forever."

"What if I don't do it? You gonna farm this out for someone else to take care of?"

His expression was blank when he responded. "No. Because knowing that Giles bastard is knocking around your mother is enough to make you homicidal. You'll kill him eventually, but you'll do it without the fifty grand, a solid plan, and a way out. How would your mama like spending her Saturdays driving back and forth to the prison to have fifteen minutes to talk with you at the state pen?"

His words painted the picture as effectively as if he held a brush in his hand like a master artist. Giles's brother, who was the DA, and their dirty cop of a sheriff would never let me get away with it. Hell, they wouldn't rest until they saw me get the lethal injection.

"Kane, you should think on this. If you're gonna do it anyway, this is the smartest option."

This came from Jeremiah, whose advice I normally trusted. But how the fuck could I trust this guy I'd never met?

"Can't believe you brought him here."

Mount interrupted. "You've got three minutes, and I'm running out of patience."

What the fuck am I doing even considering this? I asked myself.

"Who the hell are you, anyway?" I asked him.

"Lachlan Mount."

"Should I have heard of you?"

The grin that tugged at his lips could only be

described as feral. "No, because you don't exist in my world. But you take this deal, and you'll have yourself a seat at the table in it, even though you'll be a ghost. The way I see it, you have two choices—prison, or a life you can't even imagine. No more getting paid pennies for putting your ass on the line every day. No one making decisions for you but you."

"And you," I pointed out.

"For now. I don't need a fucking pet, Savage. I need a trigger man who doesn't owe anything to anyone and has the balls to take a shot no one else would dare. According to your friend here, that's you. You have one minute to decide. You in or out? Because either way, the rest of your life changes right now."

CHAPTER 4

Kane

One month before the funeral

"**W**HAT THE HELL DID YOU JUST SAY?"

Temperance, the woman I knew I shouldn't have touched, stands in front of me trying to comprehend the bomb I just dropped into her lap. A ticking time bomb, much like the one Mount tossed at me all those years ago. It never blew up in my face, but I know this one will.

"I took a contract to kill your brother. A half million. I have thirty days to complete it before it goes back out to bid."

Her eyes narrow and her posture goes rigid. "You piece-of-shit motherfucker!" She charges forward, bending to slam her shoulder into me like a linebacker. Someone should have told her not to try hand-to-hand combat with a man trained in it by the best.

I reach around her body to subdue her, but I underestimate just how wiry and agile she is as she twists and reaches for something on the coffee table.

The last thing I want is for her to go for a gun I haven't already found and unloaded. Who knew one woman would be so heavily armed? Then again, considering who her brother is, I'm not all that surprised.

But she doesn't go for a gun. She slaps the wood, palming a pen, and slashes it toward my jugular.

"Jesus fucking Christ, woman." I shackle her wrist with one hand and twist her arms in front of her body, squeezing until she has no choice but to drop the pen.

"I'm going to kill you!"

"You're not the first person to say that, and you sure as hell won't be the last."

"Yes, I will be, because I'm not going to fail." She snarls the words as I lock her hands in front of her waist, trapping her.

"You about done?"

It's the wrong question to ask. Temperance throws her head back, slamming it into my chin before sweeping my legs out from under me. We both go down hard on the wood floor.

She attempts to crawl away from me, but I grab one of the rips in the knees of her jeans to slow her down. It tears further as she kicks at my face.

"Calm the fuck down."

Again, the wrong thing to say to a woman bent on homicide. Her head swivels like she's looking for another weapon, and I use her momentary inattention to launch myself over her, landing chest to chest.

She lets out a scream that would make an Amazon proud. She swings a hammer fist toward the side of my head, and I catch her wrists in either hand and pin them to the floor.

"Let me go," she says through gritted teeth.

"Not gonna happen."

"Then kill me, because that's the only way you'll be able to walk the streets without looking over your shoulder for the rest of your life. I'll never quit hunting you."

The vehemence in her tone takes me by surprise—as does the fact that her threats make me rock hard.

"You're sexy as fuck when you're threatening to end me."

Her nostrils flare, and for the third time in as many minutes, I realize I've said the wrong thing.

This is what happens when you've spent more time in your own head than talking to people in the last fifteen years. My social skills, which were never great, have gone to shit. I'm usually content to grunt or type my response to someone's question, but Temperance has fucked up my life in more ways than she realizes.

She bucks her hips, no doubt trying to get me off her, but all she does is grind my hard dick into her crotch.

"I wouldn't do that if I were you."

Her furious brown eyes narrow. "You'll never get away with this. I don't care who you are. Once Mount finds out, *he'll destroy you.*"

"That's where you're wrong. Mount already knows."

Her face blanches, like all the blood has drained away. "What?" she whispers, blinking several times in rapid succession. "That . . . that's not possible."

"I told him when he called, asking me to come."

"But—"

"But nothing. You ready to stop trying to kill me for two minutes so I can let you up? If not, I'll stay right here as long as I need to."

Her cheeks regain a flush of color as soon as she realizes my hard-on is notched against her pussy.

"Nothing you haven't felt before, princess."

She bares her teeth like a wild thing. "I can't believe I let you—"

"Fuck you six ways to Sunday? You should probably add in there that you can't believe you liked it so fucking much."

"I hate you."

For some reason, that actually makes me smile. "Haven't you heard that love and hate are two sides of the same coin? I bet I could get you there too. Maybe just tell you that I don't intend to bury a bullet in your brother's head."

Her mouth falls open and she blinks repeatedly. "You're not going to kill him?"

"We go back a long time, and even though he obviously fucked the wrong person over in a big goddamn messy way, I don't end people I like. The list is short enough as it stands. I don't need to go scratching names off it for no good reason. Although, I guess I have five hundred thousand good ones when it comes to him."

"I don't understand. You said—" Temperance shakes her head as though she's having comprehension issues.

I shift as her hips relax. "I took a hit. Exclusive contract. That means no one else can take the job and get paid for it unless I don't complete it within thirty days."

"And you're not going to kill him." She breathes a sigh of relief, but it's way too soon for that.

"Don't go thinking Rafe is out of the line of fire yet. He got himself into some bad shit, and if we get him out of this, I might still beat him to death for being so fucking stupid. That's what gets people killed. Add on top of that all the extra work he's made for me, and the fact Mount had to get involved, he'll be lucky to keep his hide intact."

"Who wants him dead?"

I shake my head. "I'm not telling you shit, because I'm sure you'll have your little geek-squad hacker friend go trying to run them down, and then they'll know we're coming for them. I'm playing this the smart way."

"Let me up. Please."

I meet Temperance's warm brown eyes, which are drained of the urge to murder me. At least, for now. She'll probably want to kill me again later. I haven't told her everything yet.

I wouldn't be much of a hit man if I revealed all my secrets.

CHAPTER 5

Temperance

WHEN THE MAN IN MY APARTMENT ROLLS OFF me, so many thoughts are running through my head, I'm not sure how to deal with all of them.

Scratch that. Any of them.

As I turn my back on him and attempt to gather myself, I focus on the facts.

Someone put out a hit on my brother.

This guy—the one I know *biblically*, but don't know his actual name—knows my brother.

Mount knows that he accepted a hit to kill my brother.

Because he's a freaking *hit man*.

And I just turned my back on a killer.

I whip around to face him, and his expression is

hard to read. If I had to guess, I'd say a mix of amusement, approval, and . . . arousal? Since apparently I caught him on the tail end of adjusting himself.

"You go back a long time with Rafe?"

For some reason, this is one piece of the bomb-dropping revelations I'm having the most trouble digesting. Right up there with the fact that he *kills* people. Of all the possible people in all the world, how is it that I end up banging a guy who kills people *and* knows my brother?

Seriously. This. Isn't. Fair.

He nods, and it seems he's back to his man-of-few-words persona.

"How long?"

"Long enough."

I stare at him harder, like if I had the ability to shoot laser beams from my eyes, they'd be glowing red right now. "And you knew who I was the whole time?"

His face is completely impassive now. "Does it matter?"

Is he insane?

"Yes, it goddamned matters. I thought I was having some wild fling with a hot stranger, and I find out I'm banging my brother's friend!" His lips quirk like he's trying not to laugh, and my rage from earlier returns. "Don't you dare smile at me."

"Hot stranger, eh?"

"Shut up. This isn't funny."

"But you're so fucking sexy when you're furious. If I'd only known . . ."

"You would've told me who you were and pissed me off sooner?"

The mirth in his expression evaporates. "No. If it were up to me, you never would've known." His gaze intensifies. "I knew then I never should've touched you."

"Then why did you?"

His stare rakes over me, and as pissed and scared and confused as I am, I can't help but feel the rising heat. I force it away to focus on what really matters.

"I don't understand any of this. You've gotta break it down for me. Why would someone want to kill Rafe?"

"We need to move this conversation elsewhere. Somewhere safer."

This throws me for a loop. "What do you mean?"

"Pack your bag, princess. You're coming with me. Your boss's orders. Or should I say, *the* boss's orders."

He doesn't have to explain who he's talking about, but that doesn't mean I'm going to take him at face value either. I'm finally starting to understand this man is anything but what he seems on the surface.

"Don't expect me to believe a damn thing you say to me ever again." I snatch up my phone and turn to head for the bedroom.

Why did I turn my back on a killer?

I spin around, keeping my gaze locked on his face as I walk backward, my other arm stretched out behind me, feeling for my bedroom door. I shove it open and slip inside, never breaking our stare.

"Go ahead. Call her. Trust, but verify."

"Trust? That's rich." I push the door shut, cutting off my view inch by inch.

My mouthwateringly sexy view. His hair is ruffled from rolling around on the floor with me, and his collar is open.

No, Temperance. Stop. You are not interested. I laugh to myself. Even I don't believe me. Then I remind myself he's a hit man. *Sobering.*

I tap Keira's contact and wait for her to pick up.

"Did he find you?" she asks instead of a greeting.

"If by *he* you mean the hit man who took the job to kill my brother, even though he knows him? Yes. Yes, he did. Can you please tell me what the hell is going on, and what I'm supposed to do now?"

"Hold on. Lachlan wants the phone."

Of course he does, the bossy bastard, I think,

because I wouldn't dare say that out loud.

"Temperance." His deep voice sounds more relaxed than normal, which seems completely at odds with the situation at hand.

"There's a hit man in my living room," I blurt out.

"Good. Do what he says."

"Are you joking? Because I'm really, really hoping you're joking."

All I hear is silence at the other end of the call.

"Okay, so that's a hard *no* to joking. Got it." I try to inject some humor into my voice.

"Your brother is in a bad situation. This bad situation could spill over onto you. My wife doesn't want anything to happen to you, so I made a call and now you're safe."

I swallow and try to find some words to string together in a coherent sentence at his pronouncement. "What about Rafe?"

Another beat of silence. Then, "Saxon's the best. If anyone can help Rafe, it's him."

Saxon. He has a name. I picture the man in the living room, but it doesn't fit him.

"You good?" Mount asks.

Good? Is he serious?

I answer honestly. "I don't know what I am right now."

"You're cut from the same cloth as my wife. You'll rise to the occasion."

The call ends before I can respond.

"Well, fuck," I say to the empty room.

"Pack your bag. We're moving out."

I screech and whirl around to see my stranger— Saxon—standing inside the open door to my bedroom. I didn't even hear the damn thing open.

"Don't ever do that again!"

"No promises."

I narrow my gaze on him. "How do you move so quietly, anyway?"

He shoots me a crooked grin. "Part of the job description."

CHAPTER 6

Kane

SHE'S TEMPTING AS HELL, AND I CAN'T STOP watching her as she works through the information I've dropped in her lap. Temperance is either going to comply . . . or make another move to try to kill me. Jury's still out, despite Mount's orders.

These days, I only work for the unofficial king of New Orleans when it's unavoidable, or if it's a job I'd take regardless who's offering it. Mount and I primarily trade in favors lately, which he'd prefer we didn't. But I learned—and learned quickly—that a favor from Mount is worth more than money.

He's at the top of the short list of people alive who know who I am and what I do. A list I'm surprisingly content with adding Temperance Ransom to as well.

Her brother is on it. Rafe Ransom and I go back a long time, but we're not friends. I don't have friends.

The intermediary I work through on the dark web is a nameless, faceless avatar who doesn't know anything about me other than my ability to deliver on my contracts with perfect consistency.

Then there's Jeremiah, the one who set me on this path by calling Mount in the beginning. He watches out for my ma, making sure she's got what she needs. I funnel money into his accounts through cryptocurrency so it can't be traced back to my network of offshore companies.

"Where are we going?"

I keep catching myself wanting to smile around Temperance, which is completely foreign to me. I didn't even know my lips were capable of doing it so often, and I'm now actively trying to remain stone-faced. Another new challenge.

"Somewhere safe."

She draws in a long, slow breath and releases it. "Any more details you care to share?"

"No." I fight to keep from smiling again when she narrows her eyes and faces me with her hands propped on her hips. "Bring everything you need. You won't be coming back for a while."

"You know I have to work, right? I can't just go

into hiding somewhere and let the distillery go to hell. Keira's counting on me."

"They'll be back sooner than they planned. But until then, to everyone at the distillery, I'm your newly hired assistant."

"Until I fire your ass," she snaps.

I lose the battle, and a predatory smile curves my lips. "I think you should be more concerned about your ass."

Her face turns red at the reminder of our encounters at the club, which sends a punch of lust to my gut.

Can't touch her. Not here. It's not safe.

I force the thought out of my mind and ask, "Where's your bag?"

Instead of replying, she snatches a small carry-on out of the closet behind her.

I eye it skeptically. "You're telling me you can fit everything in that?"

"Don't worry. I have a duffel bag for my guns."

I speak without thinking, something I rarely do. "Who knew you were the perfect woman?"

"Yeah. Right." She flips me the bird and starts packing.

She has no idea I'm telling the truth. She is fucking perfect.

Determined. Sassy. Gorgeous. Fucks like a dream.

My instincts war with my self-control because all I want to do right now is bend her over the bed and—

Fucking stop, man. Not yet. Get her out of here first.

Fifteen minutes later, I'm stunned that she's packed and ready to go.

"So, where to? The bat cave?"

My lips twitch.

Did I mention she was fucking perfect?

CHAPTER 7

Temperance

"I'M NOT PUTTING IT ON. YOU'RE INSANE."

"Don't make me sedate you."

Even though he looks somewhat amused, I'm one hundred percent certain he's not joking.

I glance down at the beanie in my hand. The one I'm supposed to wear pulled down over my eyes so I can't see the entrance to the bat cave. I thought I was being pushed to my limit when I had to agree that he'll come back for my Bronco tomorrow, but this is some bullshit.

"What if we pull up next to a cop? He's going to think I'm being abducted. How are you going to explain that?"

Instead of duct-taping my mouth shut and

zip-tying my hands and feet, which I assume would have been standard operating procedure for a hit man—if he doesn't shoot you first—Saxon has been strangely patient.

Saxon. I still don't think the name fits him as he stares at me from the other side of the bench seat of his perfectly restored International Harvester Scout.

The waves of envy beating against the walls of my soul over his four-wheel drive may have helped my compliance when he opened the passenger door for me to climb in. But even the incredible reupholstered black-and-white bench seat that makes me yearn for the extra cash to restore my Bronco doesn't make me compliant enough to put this beanie on without argument.

He presses a button on the dash and the clear windows turn black. "Problem solved."

"Are you kidding me?" My mouth drops open, and I swivel around to look in the backseat. Every piece of glass is now tinted like a limo. "Where are the rockets mounted?"

I give him hardcore side-eye and catch a restrained chuckle from his side of the vehicle.

"I'm not Batman. There aren't any rockets. My job calls for a little more subtlety."

No way this thing is unarmed. "Machine guns?

Bullet-resistant glass? Is that why you didn't let me open the door, the weight of the armor?"

"Put. It. On."

His patience is waning, and even though I should be scared of him, I'm not. My chin juts out stubbornly.

"This is going to end in you conscious or unconscious, Temperance. You choose."

I glare. "You're a dick."

"You like my dick," he shoots back.

I hate that he's one hundred percent correct about that, so I lie.

"*Did.* Past tense. That was before I knew it was connected to a hit man." When my statement drains any humor from his expression, part of me wishes I could take it back.

"Put it on."

"Fine."

I pull the beanie over my head and cover my eyes. I don't know what kind of fabric this hat is made out of, probably the same stuff as the bat suit, but it definitely blocks all light—not to mention it smells incredible. Like him.

A spicy, clean masculine scent overwhelms me as he shifts the SUV in drive and pulls out onto the street. For a while, I try to keep track of the turns, but after about five minutes, it becomes impossible.

"Tell me about the distillery," he says. "What's coming up? More special events that are going to bring in big crowds?"

"We're running a speed-dating event this week. Professional singles are getting together in the restaurant to mix and mingle. No other events planned beyond our regular tours until next weekend, thank the Lord, or else I'd lose my mind."

"Is that your main job? Special events?"

"Technically, I'm the COO."

"Fancy title. What does it really mean?"

I roll my eyes, but he can't see them under the beanie. "That I do whatever Keira tells me to, including events. Although, we're hopefully hiring someone specifically to handle those, because it's getting to be a little overwhelming to keep up."

"You did a good job with the auction."

I shrug. "Because I had to. It was a great cause. But chasing down every last-minute detail to make sure an event goes off without a hitch isn't what I want to be doing with my life." For a moment, I wonder how smart it is to say that to someone who has a direct line to my boss's husband, but I highly doubt he's going to tattle.

"What do you want to be doing with your life?"

I'm surprised he asks, but then again, he's been a surprise in every way I can imagine.

I consider his question, and my mind immediately goes to the unfinished piece in Elijah's shop. That's not something I'm ready to share with him, so I change the subject.

"This thing itches, and it's hot." I adjust the beanie as I lie.

"You'll live."

"Are you sure?"

"Considering that's my job? Yes."

I frown, but his comment conjures another question in my brain. "How does one actually get into the hit-man line of work? Is there an apprenticeship for that?" Not the smoothest change of subject, but I don't care.

He's quiet for long moments, making me wish I could see his face.

"It wasn't my first choice."

"Army or marines?"

Although I can't see his head swivel to stare at me, I can feel it. I had a gut feeling and went with it.

"Why do you say that?"

"Your posture. I can always spot it. I had a crush on an ROTC guy in college. He carried himself like you."

"What's his name?" he asks, aiming for a casual tone, no doubt, and almost succeeding.

I choke on a laugh. "Are you really going to hunt him down because his posture gave you away?"

"Depends."

"On what?"

"How far that crush went."

I'm not sure why I like the subtle flare of jealousy, but I do.

"Where'd you go to college?" he asks next.

I pause before answering. "Don't ask me questions you already know the answer to. It's disingenuous."

"If you think I know your entire life story, you're wrong. Ransom didn't exactly go out of his way to fill me in on all the details about his baby sister—and I haven't dug that deep."

Why am I equal parts glad and annoyed at his reply? Did I want him to stalk me? I must be damaged.

"What did he tell you?" I ask to fill the growing silence.

Again, I have to wait for an answer, and I wonder if it's because he's navigating traffic or forming a reply. It feels like we're merging onto the expressway.

"Enough. You're younger. Went to college and he didn't. Work for Mount's woman. You're off-limits."

"Off-limits?" My brother isn't exactly the most

protective sibling on the planet, but he definitely scared off his fair share of guys.

I can feel Saxon's stare on me.

"Yeah. Off-limits."

So many questions fight for supremacy in my brain, but one triumphs. "Then why did you . . ." I let my words trail off.

"Next question." His reply is curt.

Something like victory bubbles up inside me, and I have no idea what to do with that feeling. We're both quiet for a few minutes before I realize I'm losing my chance to find out more about him . . . I mean, interrogate him.

"What about you? Did you enlist after high school?"

"Yes."

"Go to college at all?"

"No." His short answers aren't exactly inviting more questions.

"What was your job?"

He pauses like he might not answer. Finally, he replies, "Sniper."

"I guess that fits. How long were you in?"

"Long enough."

His non-answers should dissuade me from asking more questions, but I'm not losing my opportunity.

"Why'd you get out? Didn't like it?"

He grunts. "It was time."

"So, how'd you come to work for Mount?"

"I don't."

"Wait. I'm confused. I thought—"

"No. I don't work for anyone, and I sure as hell wouldn't take his orders every day."

"I still don't get it."

He grunts like he doesn't want to answer, but he eventually speaks again. "I'm doing him a favor. I don't pass up the chance to have Mount in my debt too often. Never know when I'll need to call it in."

I'm not sure what to make of all this, but I keep questioning him. "How do you know Rafe?"

"Through Mount," he replies, keeping his answers short, but this one brings my questions full circle.

"What did my brother do? What was so different about this job? Mount made it sound worse than normal . . ." I pause, not sure what else to say.

"How much do you know about what your brother does?"

The question catches me off guard, mostly because I never talk about it to anyone. Not just because I don't want him to get in trouble, but also because it allows me to pretend that my brother isn't a smuggler who spends more time on the wrong side of the law than the right side.

"Enough," I say, keeping my answers short like he does.

"Keep going."

"He transports things," I say, and I can almost feel the sidelong glance.

"Your brother's a transporter."

"I know. I'm not an idiot. Illegal jobs pay more than legal ones, so he takes those more often than not."

"And that bothers you?"

"It's not my life or my decision. That's on Rafe." I pause. "But if it were your brother, wouldn't it bother—" I cut my question off because I realize it's a ridiculous thing to ask a hit man.

Saxon pretends he doesn't notice. "Ransom took a big job. What, exactly, we don't know yet, but he fucked the wrong people over. The kind of people you don't want to fuck over because you won't live to tell about it."

My brain races, and fear for Rafe takes up residence all the way to the marrow of my bones. "Why would he risk screwing someone over? He should know better. He told me it was big, so it's not like he didn't know."

"Don't know, but I'm hoping he had a good

fucking reason."

Quietly, I say, "He missed my birthday. He swore he wouldn't miss it, and he did. He might not be the most upstanding person in the world, but he's all I have. And he always keeps his word."

Once again, I feel Saxon's eyes on me.

"When was your birthday?"

Even though I can't look down and see anything because of this dumb hat, my chin drops to my chest. "Today," I whisper.

"Shit. You're kidding."

I shake my head. "No. Happy freaking birthday to me."

I hate sounding like I'm throwing a pity party, but it can't be helped. Other than Keira's text this morning, not a single other soul on this planet has wished me happy birthday. How pathetic is that?

"Jesus, I'm sorry, Temperance."

"Don't worry about it. It doesn't matter. Nothing does besides making sure Rafe is okay. So, whatever I need to do to make that happen, Saxon, I'll do it."

I stop for a moment and think.

"Is that even your real name?"

CHAPTER 8

Kane

S AXON . . . THE ALIAS I PICKED OUT OF A DAMN history book in Jeremiah's back room while I waited for the go-ahead to pull the trigger on my first kill not sanctioned by the US government. I thought it sounded cool at the time—thought all of it sounded like a good idea—but I was a twenty-one-year-old punk who didn't know shit.

For the first time in a long time, I hate the name I chose. I don't want to hear it on her lips.

Only two people who know I'm alive know my real name, and I didn't realize until right now how much I want to hear someone say it after going so long without. I don't want this woman calling me by the same name killers and criminals use. I sure as hell don't want her saying it while I'm inside her.

"Kane."

As soon as I say it aloud, I know I should want to take it back. She could use it against me. Somehow find out who I am. Dredge up my past and my true identity, which need to stay buried. She has her hacker friend, and telling Temperance the truth makes me a fucking idiot.

"Kane." She tries it out, and suddenly it doesn't feel like the wrong choice. It feels like the best choice I've made in a long damn time. "I like it."

I don't know why her approval matters to me, but that feels good too.

What the hell is wrong with me? I knew she'd fucked my world upside down before, just by walking into that office scene at the club, but I didn't realize how much until now.

I like this girl.

The implications of that are inconceivable. I don't get to have relationships like normal people. I'm not normal. I've never had that luxury. Sure, I could move onto a suburban block and wave to my neighbors as they leave for work in the morning, but after a while, they'll ask too many questions and I'll have to walk away and never look back, and that kind of disappearance raises too many questions. So I keep to myself. It's safer. Easier.

"Where are you taking me, Kane?"

As soon as Temperance asks the question, I change my mind again. I definitely fucked up. She can ask me anything now, and as long as she uses my name, I'll want to answer it.

Be smart. Think with your head and not your dick. Or anything else that doesn't keep you alive.

I give her the most basic answer, which actually happens to be the truth. "My place."

"The bat cave?"

The shot of panic that punched me in the gut two seconds ago dissipates completely. "I have some cool shit, but unfortunately, no secret water entrance."

"That's disappointing. But since your name isn't Bruce, I'll let it slide."

"Thanks."

"But you have to make me a deal. If you get one, you have to let me see it without the beanie on."

I have no idea how she's keeping her sense of humor intact, but I like that too. "Deal."

"Good. Maybe we should shake on it, and then you'll trust me enough to take this dumb hat off before I suffocate."

"Not happening."

"But—"

"It's not covering your mouth. You're fine."

With a *pfft*, she blows a stream of air from her lips and a loose tendril of hair flutters by her neck, a neck I want to run my tongue—

Damn it. I need to stop noticing all the details about her.

Yeah, like that's possible. I'm hooked on this woman. *Bad.*

CHAPTER 9

Temperance

TEN MINUTES LATER, THE SCOUT SLOWS AND MY senses perk up again. They've been lulled by the sound of the tires on the highway and the surprisingly companionable silence.

We make a few more turns before he brakes, and I hear what sounds like a garage door. He accelerates again and the sound repeats, and I assume we're inside when he puts the SUV in park and turns it off.

"Is Alfred here?" I ask as I tug the hat off my sweaty head without waiting to ask permission. I'm not sure why I'm stuck on the Batman jokes. Batman wasn't a criminal hit man with a voyeuristic streak like the man sitting next to me. Although . . . maybe Bruce Wayne wasn't all that far off from Kane.

Kane. That name suits him much better than

Saxon, but I can't help but wonder if it's another alias or the name he was born with, and I need to know.

"No Alfred."

"Bummer." I turn to check out my surroundings through the tinted windows, but it's hard to see much. The little I can see sets my envy soaring, however. "You have got to be kidding me."

It's like I died and went to vintage four-wheel-drive heaven. My jaw slack, I scramble out of the Scout—and I was right about the armored door. It's heavy as hell, but it doesn't slow me down. I'm way too excited.

This is a full-blown warehouse, and it's packed with show-quality, completely restored Scouts, Broncos, Land Cruisers, Hummers, Jeeps, and more.

"Is this even real? Did you actually knock me unconscious and I'm dreaming about paradise?"

The floor is painted a slick black with red racing stripes down the center. Back in one corner are two hydraulic lifts, enough toolboxes and shiny tools to give a mechanic a woody, and what looks like an acre of shelves holding parts.

"You like it?"

I whip around to face him. "Are you insane? This is . . . this has to be one of the largest private collections of antique four-wheel drives in the country."

One corner of his mouth climbs. "In the world, actually."

"I think I'm in love."

The other corner rises. "So that's what it takes."

"With the cars," I say, clarifying.

He breaks our stare and glances out over his collection in a manner that I would expect a king to use to survey his adored subjects.

"How many are there?"

"Here? A hundred fourteen. But I have over four hundred, total."

I practically choke on the number. "How?"

"Wet work pays."

One would think my awe would be dampened at the mention of the blood money he used to buy and rebuild all these beautiful vehicles. One would also be wildly wrong.

"Is this your front? How you launder money?"

He shrugs as he walks away. "Something like that. Come on."

I can't tear my gaze away from the cars, and I reach out to caress the back of one side mirror. The chrome is impeccable. Like it just rolled off the assembly line.

"Temperance." My name echoes through the massive warehouse, and he shuts the tailgate of the

Scout loud enough to catch my attention. He has my carry-on in one hand and my duffel over his shoulder.

Kane has them, I should say. *He has a name.*

My earlier question comes back to the forefront. "Is Kane really your name, or another alias?"

I'm asking a million and one questions for several reasons. One, because information is power. And two, because it's keeping my mind off freaking out about my brother. If Mount hadn't ordered me to do what Kane says, I would be demanding we go find Rafe right now. I'm saving that up for another five minutes, and then I'll be on him.

"Does it matter?"

He lowers my carry-on to sit on its wheels and opens a gate that blocks the freight elevator. It's the kind you see in movies, but I have never seen one in real life.

I step inside and wait while he closes the gate before hitting the button for the third floor. "You know my real name. It seems only fair."

He looks at me out of the corner of his eye. "Not because I've fucked you?"

"Don't remind me."

I truly mean that because if he says more, I'm going to be thinking about how badly I want him to do it again. *Which can't happen.* Not only because he's a hit man, but because I need to stay focused on Rafe.

But the incredible smell rolling off him now that we're in this enclosed space reminds me that not everything about him is terrible.

The elevator stops, and he pauses before going through the motions to let us out. "Yes. It's my real name."

There's something unspoken in that admission. Like I need to guard his real name with my life because it could really fuck up his world if I disclosed it.

I should be running to the cops with that information. To Valentina's husband, at the very least. Or even to Ariel. But I don't want to, and not only because my boss's husband would probably be the one to put a hit on me if I got them involved with this situation. Working for Keira now has something in common with growing up in the bayou—we handle things ourselves. No outsiders.

The thought flies out of my head as I take the first step out of the elevator.

Oh. My. God.

"Holy shit," I whisper.

My sculpture is sitting as a showpiece in the entryway to Kane's massive loft living space.

My sculpture. In his home.

I tear my gaze off the metal long enough to look at Kane's face. His attention is still on my work, like he's marveling over it. That hits me in places I don't want to admit.

"I had to buy it. I couldn't not."

"Did you know—" I say, but I lose my nerve.

"What?"

I rephrase. "Did you know it wasn't Gregor Standish's work?"

"I didn't care who the artist was. I just had to have it."

Pride makes me lift my chin higher and dare to tell him the truth. "It's mine."

He turns to stare at me, his gaze narrowed. "What do you mean?"

"I made it. It's my art."

He looks from me to the sculpture and back again, like he's seeing me in a new way. A way I like more than is healthy or smart.

"How the hell did I not know that?"

Casually, I shrug a shoulder. "Not many people do. It was a mistake. It wasn't supposed to be in the auction."

"I'm not giving it back," Kane says, his eyes narrowing. "It's mine."

Something in his possessive statement starts a fire low in my belly. I swallow, trying to ignore it. "I wouldn't ask you to. The donation went to a good cause."

His expression shutters again before he grunts.

We stand in silence for a few moments, both studying my artwork. I recognize the flaws in it. The welds where my technique could have been better. The piece of metal that wasn't cut cleanly. The edge that sliced open my hand when I moved it from the scrap yard.

"I can do better. I'm going to." I don't know what possesses me to make the declaration, but Kane turns to look at me again.

"Explain."

"A gallery in the Quarter commissioned several pieces. I have to work on them this week. My skills will get sharper. I'll get better. Someone's actually going to pay for those pieces."

"I paid for this one."

"But it wasn't intended for sale. It was just . . . me screwing around. I could've welded this part better." I point out the piece that's bothering me.

"The imperfections make it unique. Don't ever apologize for those."

I soak up his words as he lowers my duffel onto a

console table by the elevator.

"Come on. I'll give you a tour, if you'd like to see the place."

I latch onto the distraction before I do something stupid, like jump him. "Turn down a chance to see the bat cave? Never."

He grunts again as he leads me through the massive cavernous space. It's wide open, with huge windows on two sides tinted black to prevent anyone from seeing in from the outside.

"What was this place?"

"Storage."

"I know we're still in New Orleans. So if you're trying to ensure I never know where your hideout is, it's probably not going to work."

"I can try."

"You forget, I have GPS on my phone." I feel smug as I point out the flaw in his plan.

One side of his mouth quirks up. "Won't work within a quarter-mile radius of the building, but good try, princess."

I shrug like it's no big deal and survey the large kitchen that seems to have a square mile of granite countertops. The fancy appliances may as well have price tags on them, because they scream *expensive*.

"You're loaded, aren't you?" It's a stupid question,

especially because of the comment he made downstairs about the cars.

"I do okay." He gestures to the kitchen. "There's food in the fridge and cupboards. Help yourself. If you like to cook, feel free. If you want something I don't have, ask."

He doesn't wait for a response before continuing toward the living area. "Living room. TV has satellite and everything else you could imagine." I follow him as he stops in front of a wide-open staircase. "Bedrooms and bathrooms are on the top level."

I soak in everything I can see. The decor is clearly of the industrial persuasion, which works for the space. The black leather couches look comfortable, like I could curl up and take a nap right now. That is, if there were any pillows or a blanket. The place is devoid of female touches and there's not a single picture of a person, but he does have framed photographs of landmarks around the world hanging on the wall, along with canvases and masks and weapons. I can't help but wonder if he took the pictures himself.

Then there are the shelves holding a wide array of items I can't even begin to list without a closer look. *Travel souvenirs?*

Kane crosses to a large metal-and-wood cabinet.

"Drink?" he asks as he splashes what looks like whiskey or Scotch into a tumbler, no ice.

Given the day I've had, I'm not saying no, even though hard liquor isn't my thing. "Make mine a double." It's something I've always wanted to have the chance to say.

When he carries two glasses over to the table in front of the sofa, he jerks his chin as if to summon me. He's got the booze, so I go. I take one tumbler from him, and before I can raise it to my lips, he clinks the rim.

"I know this isn't ideal, but happy birthday, Temperance."

The birthday wish is a reminder of everything wrong in my world, also known in general as *every damn thing*. I look over at the sculpture in his entryway and amend my thought. *Almost everything.*

"Thanks." My voice still carries a rough edge.

"Tell me what Rafe told you before he left."

I wrap both hands around the glass before sinking onto the luxurious leather cushion of the sofa. His question brings me back to what matters most—my brother.

"That he had a big job. A dangerous one."

"He didn't give specifics?"

"Would you tell your sister?" I ask after taking a

sip. Warmth rolls over my tongue.

"If I had a sister, I'd make sure nothing ever touched her."

No sister, then.

"To do that, Rafe would have to cut me off completely, and that's not something I'd ever forgive him for doing." A wave of emotion washes over me, and sudden tears burn behind my eyes. "Not that I'll ever forgive that bastard for taking such stupid chances with his life."

Kane reaches out and covers my knee with his wide palm. "He's a grown man. Capable. He knows what the hell he's doing." He squeezes, but I notice he makes no promises about getting Rafe back safely.

"Then why would he screw someone over? He has to know that couldn't end well."

Kane's lips flatten out. "Your brother doesn't exactly ask a lot of questions before he takes a job. Especially if the price is right."

I take another gulp of liquor, and the heat burns a path to my belly. Dropping my head back on the cushion behind me, I close my eyes. "Stupid or greedy. Those are the two reasons someone screws up, right?"

Kane nods.

"So, which is it?"

"Can't tell you. Because there might be another alternative."

"Like what?"

"Maybe he found that line he wouldn't cross."

I snort. "Right. The man who'll smuggle anything if the price is right suddenly has morals."

He looks at me strangely. "You think your brother will smuggle anything?"

"I assume so."

Kane shakes his head. "First off, from what I know, Rafe doesn't take every job that comes his way. He can pick and choose, just like me. He might work a lot, but he's choosy all the same."

I'm not sure if that makes me feel better or worse. "So, what's the next step? Kill the people who are trying to kill him? Find him before they do?"

Kane tosses back the rest of his liquor. "We dig. Then we react."

The generic reply doesn't exactly fill me with comfort.

"How long does Rafe have to realistically stay safe? You said you have an exclusive contract for thirty days. Then what?"

CHAPTER 10

Kane

TEMPERANCE IS AN ANOMALY. SHE SHOULD BE crying and begging me to find her brother. Offering up anything and everything to get Rafe back right this very minute. The fact that she's not tells me a hell of a lot.

First off, she's far more aware of how Rafe's world works than I realized, even though I know he keeps her on the periphery. Her questions are pointed and intelligent.

All of this just makes me want her more.

Over the last fifteen years, I've convinced myself that no woman walking this earth, except possibly one in my same line of work, could fit into my life or overlook what I do. I definitely shouldn't be thinking that Temperance could, but based on this limited amount of information, I am.

"Depends. Rafe's good at disappearing. He knows those swamps better than most, I'd say, and if he doesn't want to be found, he won't be for a long damn time."

She rubs her face. "So, how does this work? What's the real threat?"

I give it to her straight. "If they can't get to Rafe, they'll try to use you to draw him out. They'll kill you both. If they find him before we come up with a plan, they'll kill him."

"So, what the hell is the plan, and when are you coming up with it?"

"I'm working on it."

"I'm not second-guessing your skills, but it sounds like there's a whole hell of a lot up in the air right now."

"There is, but Mount called me in to keep you safe. You're not part of this. You don't need to suffer for what your brother did."

"But you have to keep him safe too. I can't . . . I can't lose him. Rafe's all I have left."

I can't tell her that there's very little chance this is going to work out with a happily-ever-after.

"Can't you just kill all the bad people, and then he can come back?"

I meet her gaze. "We keep you out of their hands, and I'll work on Rafe. That's all I can do."

When she tips back the rest of her liquor, I rise and retrieve the decanter to refill her glass, and then splash another measure into mine.

"That's the plan, then? Wait and see? Why not hunt them down?"

I don't answer, and she somehow works it out in her head.

"Oh, wait. That's not the job you're getting paid to do."

"I'm not getting paid for this job. Mount owes me a favor now."

"You know what I mean."

We both go quiet, sipping our drinks and no doubt considering similar things.

"I can't make you any promises, except I'll do what I can, and at the end of the day—*you* will be safe."

She studies me for long moments. She must realize that's all she's going to get from me, so she nods. "Okay."

Now I have to change the subject before she twists herself up about this anymore. There's nothing either of us can do tonight. I've put out the word I need carried, and now I wait.

"How did you start making metal sculptures?" I ask.

The question has been hovering in my subconscious since she confessed to being the artist of the piece I bought. I would have made the donation to Mary's House regardless, but the piece hooked me. Once I saw it, I had to own it. Knowing Temperance made it . . . that made both it and her even more incredible.

Temperance's gaze drops to the liquor in her glass as if it's the most fascinating thing in the entire world. "When you grew up how I did, there weren't a lot of options to keep a kid busy. Rafe loved to hunt and fish and explore the swamp. He told me a story about an eighteen-foot gator he saw and scared the hell out of me one summer. I wouldn't get in a boat for months, no matter how much my dad yelled at me. Instead, I hung around his workshop and collected scrap metal, and started to put it together to make stuff. Eventually, when I got older, I learned to solder and then weld, and it kind of took on a life of its own. I never intended to sell it. It didn't occur to me that people would pay, especially that kind of money, for things like that."

I think about how much all the other bidders had been willing to pay. Temperance's work has a market.

There's no doubt about that.

"And now that you have? What does that mean for your job at Seven Sinners?"

She looks up at me from beneath long, dark eyelashes. "I'm pretty sure this is a case of *don't quit your day job*." She smiles, but it looks more like a grimace.

"But you don't sound like you love your day job." To myself, I add, *and you don't light up when you talk about it like you do your art.*

"Parts of it," she says, correcting me.

"So even if you make enough to live on from your sculptures, you're going to keep working at the distillery?"

She pauses like she hasn't even considered the possibility. "It's not a reliable source of income. Plus, it's not as respectable as being a COO."

Her response surprises me. "Respectable? Really? You give a shit about that?"

Her eyes narrow on me. "You try being bayou trash and tell me how it feels."

Ahhh. And another piece of the puzzle that is the fascinating Temperance Ransom falls into place. "So you'd keep a job you don't like over quitting to do what you love, just because of what other people think?"

"You don't get it." She takes another sip.

"No, I guess I don't. After all, I'm pretty sure I don't have what you'd call a respectable job, and it doesn't bother me a damn bit. Actually, fuck respectability and what anyone else thinks. It doesn't matter. Having a respectable job doesn't make someone a good person."

CHAPTER 11

Temperance

KANE'S ANSWER IS MIND-BLOWING. HE'S A *HIT man*. He kills people for a living. How can he not care what people would think of that? Then again, it's not something he probably tells many people, but still.

"You do have a point, I guess."

To that, he says nothing, just drinks contemplatively. I take a cue from him and do the same.

When my glass is empty, the heat from the bourbon is flowing in my veins and I feel a lot more mellow. *Maybe this is why people drink. It takes away all the bad shit.*

Normally I'm only good for one or two glasses of wine, so multiple shots of hard liquor go straight to my head.

"You should have an Alfred," I blurt.

A burst of rusty laughter gets away from him. "What's your obsession with Batman?"

"I really don't have one. I just find this whole thing to be surreal, and if you had a butler with a British accent, I'd truly believe I was dreaming."

He plucks the glass out of my hand. "I think you've had enough."

"That stuff didn't even taste that bad."

He laughs. "If you knew how much it cost, you probably would've choked on it."

"Or felt really bad when I spit it out on your nice rug. Who decorated this place, anyway?"

I scan the cavernous room—which manages to be masculine, inviting, and functional at the same time—with its exposed ductwork, metal and wood beams, expensive contemporary furniture, and ma-hogany-and-cream color scheme.

"I did."

"Wow." Although, I probably shouldn't be sur-prised, considering he probably couldn't go hire an interior designer to decorate his secret hideout of a warehouse. *Bat cave still sounds cooler*. Especially now that I'm tipsy.

"One more drink," I say, not wanting to lose this feeling. In the warmth of my buzz, I'm able to let go of the worry about everything I can't control, even if only for an hour or two. Reality will descend soon enough.

"I thought you didn't drink."

I roll my eyes. "You really think my name holds true?"

"No, but you never went to the bar in the club to get a drink."

"Because I didn't know about it until Magnolia showed me. Besides, it seemed like there were some creepers there."

His brows dive together. "Who?"

"Some guy named Giles. Sounded pretentious as hell. I thought names weren't allowed there anyway, so it was weird that Magnolia let it slip."

Something flashes across Kane's expression, but it's gone before I can attempt to interpret its meaning. Not that I'm in top form, or really good at reading the tiny things his expression gives away at all.

But I want to be.

That thought rocks my foundation. I'm already grappling with the fact that I still have a serious case of lust for a hit man, and now I'm threatened with maybe *liking* the guy. I shouldn't want to know him better.

My rational brain intrudes with a counterargument. *Your brother is a criminal who apparently ripped off some very bad people. Does that make you love him less?*

Touché, brain. Touché.

"If I could read minds . . ." His deep voice interrupts my train of thought.

"What?"

"I was thinking I would learn a hell of a lot of interesting stuff if I could read yours."

I shake my head but the realization stays stuck. I could *like* a hit man. *That's not happening.*

So I lie, which is something I seem to do all too often around him tonight. "Not really. It's mostly boring in there."

"Not with as often as you must think about me naked," he says with a wicked grin.

Images of him flashing the same wicked grin as he stalked toward me at the club dominate my mind, and I mumble, "Well, I am now."

Both his eyebrows go up, and I fall further and further down the rabbit hole. He's too attractive for his own good. And when I think about what's beneath that placket of buttons and those perfectly tailored pants . . .

No. I need to stop thinking about that. I need to stop thinking about all of it. How devastating he was with his hands, his mouth, his . . .

I tip back the drink and down it all in a final gulp. "Easy there."

I ignore him and help myself to another measure of booze. I've never been the sort to find my oblivion in a bottle, but I'm starting to understand why it's such a popular solution.

Have a problem? Add alcohol, and the edges go fuzzy and your brain slows down. Still bothering you? Obviously, have a little more, or just get blackout drunk and you won't remember anything.

My better judgment pipes up to remind me that I'm in the company of a killer. *A killer with the most incredible eyes I've ever seen and the best taste in art.*

I wander away from his piercing stare and stand in front of a totem pole in the corner with an eagle's beak and wings extending from the top.

"Tell me about the rest of your art. It's a pretty eclectic collection." My tongue threatens to stumble over the last syllables, but I manage. Just barely.

"I'm a man of eclectic tastes." His tone carries a hint of suggestion, like we're not only talking about his taste in art.

"Meaning you were banging a brunette, a blonde, and a redhead all at the same time?" The question pops out, and I don't want to take it back. It's been bugging me since the night he stood me up. *Was he with another woman?*

Now I realize it's more likely that he wasn't, but I have no proof. Is it strange that I'd prefer he was out killing someone rather than having sex with another woman?

There's something seriously wrong with me.

Another laugh spills free, and this one sounds less rusty than the first. "Just one delicious brunette." His voice curls around my ear as the heat of his body penetrates the back of my blouse.

I spin around. "How do you move so freaking quietly? It's creepy. Like Edward Cullen's crazy speed." I pause, my bookish imagination going wild. "Are you a vampire?"

His entire expression softens as he throws his head back and fills the wide-open space with laughter.

"You're one of a kind, Temperance. Truly," he says, and I soak up the compliment like sunshine after a hurricane. "Any other questions?"

I open my mouth to rattle off one of the many I have, but he presses a finger to my lips.

"Never mind. I know what the answer is to that. I'll give you the answers I can. In time." He pauses, his icy blue eyes flashing like dry lightning. "But I like that you were jealous."

"I wasn't jealous."

"Liar."

He drags his finger across my bottom lip, and my tongue darts out to lick it.

"You're playing a very dangerous game, Temperance."

I like that he says my name. For some reason, it makes me feel more certain. We aren't two complete strangers anymore. He knows who I am and where I come from, and he still looks at me the same way he did before—like he wants to devour me.

"Haven't you heard? My life's a dangerous game." I don't know where that sultry, sexy voice came from as my eyelids flutter closed and I lean toward him, my lips anticipating the brush of his.

But it doesn't come.

I blink and stare at him. His features have lost their heat, turning to stone.

"It shouldn't be. You should be safe. Fuck your brother for dragging you into this. Fuck me for ever touching you. Both of us should be shot."

All my good feelings from a few moments ago dissolve, and it pisses me off. *I liked those feelings.*

I poke him in the chest with a finger. "Get off your high horse. I know what you are now, and you don't see me running in the other direction because . . .

You. Don't. Scare. Me." I punctuate each of the last four words with another poke.

Lightning flashes through his gaze again, and his jaw flexes. "So be it."

Before I can truly comprehend what's happening, he sweeps me into his arms and we're moving toward the stairs. The world spins, and I wrap my arms around his neck. Kane is a rock in the world of chaos swirling around me.

The upper level of his place is dark, but he moves with confidence. If he can see in the dark, I wouldn't be surprised. When he lowers me to my feet, I expect to be in a bedroom, but there are walls of glass and mirrors.

A bathroom?

He flips the lights on low and I see what appears to be a shower. When he steps inside and hits a few controls, steam blooms from nozzles.

Despite the warming temperature in the room, my nipples peak and my clit throbs. My inhibitions apparently faded with each shot of liquor I drank, and I reach for the buttons of my blouse.

He brushes my hands away before undoing the buttons one at a time. "When you walked into that room for the first time, I felt like I took a sledgehammer to the chest."

I lift my gaze to his.

"And when you realized what was happening in the next room? I've never seen anything so fucking sexy in my life. How badly did you want to touch yourself?"

I can't even begin to describe how badly when he's looking at me like that.

He reaches the last button and pushes the silk over my shoulders. I let it fall to the floor.

"I wanted to watch you touch yourself while you watched them. It took everything I had to stop you."

My hands go to the button of my jeans, but Kane's already there. He peels them down my legs and I stand before his crouching form, dying for him to touch me again.

"Why did you?"

"The second you touched yourself, I would've pinned you to the desk."

My nipples tighten, imagining him coming out of the shadows to take me like the man had owned that woman. The image of him fucking her face flashes across my brain. I wanted that. Now, I just want my stranger.

No, not a stranger anymore. I want Kane.

He rises to his feet before me. In his jeans and T-shirt, he's even more devastating than in the suit he wore that night. The sleeves stretch around his biceps, and every inch of ink-covered skin makes me want to trace the lines with my tongue, pushing away the clothing that hides the rest of it. He's big and forbidden, but somehow, that makes him infinitely more striking. And he's struck me so hard as to knock me completely off-balance.

He's a dangerous man. A man I shouldn't be drawn to. Shouldn't want more than I want to breathe right now. But I do. And as much as I want to throw my control at his feet, I hang on to a thread, telling myself it matters.

Taking a step toward the billowing steam, I reach behind my back to unhook my bra, shrug it down my arms, and pull it free before dropping it.

"You want to watch me now, don't you?"

"Fuck yes."

His voice sounds ragged, almost as needy as the one inside my head, and a surge of power fills me as I strip off my panties, reach back to find the glass door, and push it open. Steam envelops me, and the heat intensifies everything I'm already feeling.

"I want to watch you touch yourself too." I've thought about that more than I want to admit since that first night.

I let the door close with me inside and keep

moving back until my shoulder blades hit the tile. The hair around my face curls into tiny ringlets from the humidity, and my fingertips send chills skating across my skin when I drag them over my collarbone.

His eyes flash, and I feel like I'm taunting a wild animal. It's more intoxicating than the liquor.

"You must like dangerous games, because you're playing one again." His voice is deeper, rougher, like maybe he's half as affected by me as I am by him.

I want to make him burn for me. I want to force him to lose his grip on his iron control. What would happen if he stopped holding back and just *took*?

"I'm just getting started. Feel free to jump in whenever you'd like." I skim over my nipples, and they tighten impossibly harder before I thumb them.

Kane's nostrils flare just before he reaches behind his neck and pulls his shirt over his head and tosses it on the floor. His gaze locks on mine, saying the next move belongs to me.

Good Lord, he's ridiculously sexy. His body couldn't be more perfect if a great master carved it from stone and then added his tattoos in perfect strokes. I'm so far out of my league, it's not even funny. And yet, his big hands flex at his sides like he can barely keep himself from ripping the glass door off the shower to get to me.

Another wave of need and power wash over me, spurring me on. I circle the tight buds like I'm about to pluck them, but I don't. I'm a tease.

Kane takes a menacing step forward before he remembers his jeans and boots. The shoes go first, and then he makes quick work of the button fly. His cock pops out without briefs to hold it back, and he shoves the jeans down before kicking them aside. He takes another step forward, but instead of ripping the door open, he leans against it, his fingers splayed on the glass as he stares at me.

"You don't have any fucking idea what you do to me. You're an unholy temptation."

CHAPTER 12

Kane

TEMPERANCE, THE UNHOLY TEMPTATION. IT's exactly what she is. Maybe that's why I was so drawn to her even from the beginning, when I told myself I wouldn't touch her. But everything about her—from each strand of the thick, dark hair on her head to the smooth skin taunting me as it wraps around every curving inch of her body—was made to destroy my control.

Maybe to destroy me.

I've never wanted anything in my life as badly as I want her. And all it does is grow and spread until I'm consumed by her.

Throw in her attitude and the streak of vulnerability she tries to hide? She has no idea of the power she has over me. It's not because I'm watching her tease herself, dragging her fingertips over her nipples and back again, that I'm caught in her snare.

No. It's everything that is Temperance Ransom. She's got me by the balls.

I'm trapped. Willingly.

God help me if she ever finds out.

"Are you coming in?"

She plucks at her nipples again, and I want to tug one between my teeth and make her moan myself, but that's not what started this. I want to watch her touch herself more than I want to live to see tomorrow.

"Are you going to be a good girl when I do?"

A catlike smile curls her lips upward before they form a single word. "No."

Fuck. This woman is beyond dangerous.

The first time was supposed to be playing with fire and getting out before I got burned, but when she ran from the room, I was nowhere near ready for her to go. But still, I told myself *never again*.

Then I saw her at the auction. Saw her and watched her.

I knew I'd been lying to myself. I would have gone after her. Found a way to lure her back to the club. I should have waited. Shouldn't have met her that second night when I covered her in a blanket. It took every bit of my self-control to walk out of that room. I wanted to say *fuck it* to the job I was already late leaving for, even though it would have destroyed my reputation and possibly cost me my life.

Temperance Ransom has no idea how dangerous she is. Every man has one thing that could lead to his downfall. I've always been so fucking smug that I didn't.

Until I met her.

I should be cursing her, but all I want to do is make her feel the same storm that's raging inside me. I want her to feel this addiction.

Fuck. I want to keep her.

And that would be the final nail in my coffin. But not tonight. Tonight, we steal whatever we can get.

"Are you coming?" she asks.

Fuck yes, I think. We're both coming tonight.

I let a lazy smile stretch my lips before wiping it away, and grip the metal handle on the glass separating us. "When I open this door, you're mine. You follow my orders. Obey my commands."

Her dark eyebrows rise. "I guess we'll see if you can make me, *Kane*."

She emphasizes my name, and it unleashes another rush of need as I yank the door open.

Staring at me through her lashes, she plays with her nipples, and her tongue darts out to wet her bottom lip.

Temperance the temptress.

And all fucking mine.

CHAPTER 13

Temperance

WHEN HIS GAZE MEETS MINE AGAIN, I swallow. "I want to know how you taste when you come down my throat."

It's like unleashing a beast.

"Fuck me," he says on a groan before attacking my mouth.

There's no hesitation, only dominance. His lips crash against mine as his tongue demands entrance, and he swallows my moans and mumbled words—most likely begging. He doesn't stop until my body feels like it's on fire, and the only way to put it out is to climb him and slide down on his cock until I'm stretched so full that there's no more him and me, only us.

My hips buck against him as my right leg rises of

its own volition, wrapping around his hip, trying to force his cock against my pussy.

"I need you. Now."

He tears his lips away and lifts my chin to force my gaze up to his. "Changing your mind so quick? I thought you wanted this—" His hips flex against me, and his shaft is rock hard. "Down your throat."

"But—"

"Anyone can throw out bold words, princess. But can you back them up?"

I nod.

His blue gaze burns hotter. "Good. Because you don't get my cock until you swallow every drop of my cum and suck me until I'm hard again."

I inhale sharply, his words just as powerful as his dominating kiss.

If he thinks I'm going to back down and shy away from his dark desires, he doesn't know me that well. He doesn't know how long I've dreamed of this—a man strong enough to take control and bend me to his will, but masterful enough to make me love every second of my submission.

An alpha female only bows to a man strong enough to be worthy of her.

"Make me." I form each word with purpose. With hope. It may be perverse, but I want him to push me.

His expression blazes with approval, his pupils dilating. *He loves this.* And so do I.

His hands lock around my wrists and he leads me back toward the built-in bench. A single towel hangs on the bar above it. He reaches behind him to snag it before dropping it on the floor.

"On your knees, temptress."

He releases my wrists and I glance down at the towel, which is quickly turning damp in the thick steam. I'm shocked by his thoughtfulness. So shocked, I almost do it. But I pause, reaching down to fold the towel in a neat cushion before looking him in the eye again.

"How bad do you want me on my knees, Kane?"

His eyes flash with intensity. He understands what I need.

Kane reaches out and grips my shoulders with his huge hands. "Bad enough to put you there myself."

He increases the pressure, and I resist for only a moment before I bend. His grip tightens just before he releases me.

"Men would kill to have you on your knees before them if they had any idea how fucking incredibly beautiful you look there." He grips the base of his cock with a rough tug, but his other hand finds my chin, forcing my gaze upward. "I can feel your power rolling off you in waves. Even though you're on your knees, you still know you're in control."

His astute observation shocks me—because he's right.

I open my mouth to reply, but his thumb slides over my bottom lip and pushes inside.

"I'm still going to test your limits, temptress. Because you're trying to destroy mine. Now, suck. Show me you want my cock between these lips."

The gauntlet has been thrown. This isn't just sex, it's a decadent exchange of power and control. Give and get. Bend and receive. But I'm still determined to make him break first.

I wrap my lips around his thumb and stroke the pad with my tongue. I moan as I suck, taking it all as he pushes it deeper. I pretend it's his cock and worship it. He strokes his dick harder and harder with each second his thumb is between my lips.

I'm jealous of his fingers as he sweeps a drop of his pre-cum from the tip. My thoughts must be stamped on my face.

"You want this?"

Slowly, I nod, and he pulls his thumb free and

releases his grip on his cock to spread the wetness across my lower lip. My tongue swipes out to taste that saltiness. But it's all a tease.

I want more. I want him to push me to the edge.

CHAPTER 14

Kane

GREEDY. THAT'S EXACTLY HOW SHE LOOKS AS she licks my pre-cum off her lips.

Greed has never looked so fucking sexy.

"You want my dick? You're going to take it like a good girl?"

She nods.

"I want to hear you say it."

Temperance leans forward, presses her palms against my quads, and drags her cheek alongside my shaft, barely making contact.

Her gaze cuts to mine. "I want to see how much I can fit in my mouth."

Like before, her words are bold, but I'm bolder. I cup the side of her face.

"You're going to take every inch, even if it means

you're swallowing me down your pretty throat." Her fingers tense on my legs as I use my other hand to grasp the base of my dick and bring the head to her lips. "Lick. I want you tonguing the head like you did my thumb."

Her eyes widen, and for a moment I wonder if she'll balk again, but she smiles.

"Finally." She wraps her lips around the head and proceeds to destroy me.

CHAPTER 15

———— ✦ • ✦ ————

Temperance

I't's NOT JUST A BLOW JOB—IT'S A BATTLE OF wills. Or, at least, it is for the first minute. But when he groans out his pleasure, I completely forget about anything but hearing him make that sound again. I lick and suck and take him deeper.

"Fuck. Yes. Like that."

He holds my face, keeping me in place as his guttural sounds increase, and so does the intensity of his thrusts. He hits the back of my throat, and my eyes prick with tears as I gag. I talked a big game, but I truly have little experience in this. And somehow, Kane knows.

He strokes my cheek. "You can take it all, princess. Swallow next time. Breathe through your nose."

He pulls out and goes slower the next time,

watching me closely. I gag again and pull back, wiping at the tears on my lashes.

"You okay?"

I'm not, but I feel less powerful than I did when I was making promises with my lips that apparently my throat can't cash.

I close my eyes.

"Look at me." His tone is firm but gentle as he strokes my cheek, and I glance up at him. "If you change your mind, say so. Then we stop or switch it up. I'll never push you past a hard limit. If you aren't getting off on something we're doing, neither am I."

Something about his understanding shifts the pieces inside me, putting a jagged crack in the wall I've had in place around my heart for as long as I can remember.

"You don't have any problem telling me what you do want. The same goes for what you don't want. Got it?"

I nod again, but instead of feeling dumb, I'm calm and determined. "Would you sit down?"

He glances at the bench behind him. "Whatever you want, princess."

I smirk. "Be careful what you say."

"Not tonight." He lowers his big body onto the bench, shivering for a moment when he touches the cold tile.

"Spread your legs."

He complies with my request, and I scoot the towel forward and reposition myself.

"Say the word and I'll fuck you against the wall instead."

I shake my head. "Maybe later. I'm busy right now."

CHAPTER 16

Kane

I KNOW WHY RANSOM ALWAYS WARNED ME AWAY from his little sister. She's fucking incredible. Before, she was an addiction. Now, she's becoming something even more dangerous.

A habit.

It's no secret I like to watch. That's what I do. Study and observe.

With Temperance, though, I marvel.

From the doorway to my bedroom, I watch her sleep curled around my pillow like she was curled around me before I climbed out of bed. Or, more accurately, as I forced myself to let her go.

It's been over fifteen years since I've spent the night with a woman, and even then it wasn't sleeping with them so much as passing out drunk. I haven't wanted to be that close to someone for an entire night. But Temperance is different.

Temperance is a .50-caliber round to the head— game over.

At that thought, I force myself to turn away and get to work. With one last backward glance, I leave the sleeping woman behind to face another far less desirable subject . . .

The mess her brother made that I have to clean up.

CHAPTER 17

Temperance

T HE NEXT MORNING, I WAKE TO AN EMPTY BED and tangled sheets that aren't my own. It takes a moment of panic and confusion for me to remember where I am.

With my stranger. No, he has a name now. With *Kane*.

Memories of what we did last night come back with complete clarity, despite the alcohol I drank. Shockingly, I don't have so much as a headache, even though I tossed back the hard liquor like it was my job. Hit-man trick?

The offhand thought stops me cold.

Hit man.

My brother is a smuggler, and I've helped boost and chop cars, so it's not like I can get on my high horse and judge anyone . . . but this feels different.

Bigger. Foreign. Scary.

I've always been able to convince myself that Rafe's smuggling is a victimless crime. I know that's essentially burying my head in the sand, but it's what helps me sleep at night. I've chalked up my past life of crime to poor decision-making or necessity. After all, beggars can't be choosers, and I've fallen into the beggar category for most of my formative years.

But a hit man? That's even harder to accept in the morning light.

The scent of coffee wafts into the room as the man at the center of my thoughts steps through the threshold carrying a mug.

"I wasn't sure how you take it, so I guessed black."

He crosses the room, stopping at the edge of the bed and holding it out. I accept the warm mug and inhale the rich aroma. It smells completely different from the industrial-type brew we make at the distillery in the communal pot.

"Black works."

The mug's heat soaks into the palms of my hands as I curl them around the pottery. When I take a sip, my assumption is confirmed—it tastes like manna from heaven. As he said before, wet work pays well.

And not just well enough to afford the fancy coffee, but a massive warehouse and the world's largest collection of restored four-wheel drives.

The delicious coffee suddenly tastes a little more harsh and bitter on my tongue as I'm reminded of the blood money that bought it.

I can't stop myself from asking the question burning in my mind. "How do you live with yourself? Doing what you do?"

The warmth in Kane's expression turns to frost. He pivots and strides out of the room without a word.

Great way to start the day, Temperance.

Feeling like a complete asshole, especially when I find my clothes neatly folded on a chair, I dress and linger over the cooling coffee. I'm not sure I want to face him, and definitely uncertain whether I can apologize for the question.

I shore up my courage and carry the mug out of the bedroom, forcing myself down each stair to face him. How is that I felt so connected to him last night, but everything feels so different this morning? I should have started with asking about my brother and what progress he's made in that direction.

That's what matters.

Nothing else.

I tread carefully on the stairs and pause midway down when I spy the cluttered countertops of the kitchen.

What the hell?

Kane has his back to me while he works at the stove, but he must know I'm there because he stiffens. But all of this is secondary to the stacks of newspapers on the bar.

I glance at him and finish my trek down the stairs.

"You want an answer? How can I live with myself being a trigger man? Pick up any one of those papers and tell me the world wouldn't be better off without at least one of those sick fucks."

I cross to the first stack of papers and read the top headline.

GIRL HELD CAPTIVE FOR 16 YEARS
FINALLY SPEAKS OUT

Then the next one.

MAN RESPONSIBLE FOR MALL SHOOTING ON TRIAL

The next stack has a paper from Paris, and my French, while not perfect, comes through.

Terrorists Kill 7 by Crashing Car into Crowd

"If you don't want the hands of a killer on you, I won't blame you. I also won't apologize for what I do."

I find my voice. "So some people just need killing?" I whisper. "Is that it? It isn't about the money at all?"

"No amount of money can make me take a job if I won't be able to live with myself after it's done."

I look up at his somber face and somehow find comfort in his solemn tone.

This isn't a man who kills indiscriminately and has no care for the value of human life. He actually probably understands that value more than anyone, because he knows how it feels to pull the trigger and end it.

"I believe you." I set the coffee mug on the counter and pick up the paper to my left. The one with the headline about the girl who was held captive by a deranged man. "I would've killed this bastard myself if I'd had the chance."

His icy expression melts a few degrees.

"I'm not just saying that. I mean it."

"I believe you." He echoes my words from a few moments before.

For almost a minute, we stare at each other in silence, and I'm not certain what to say next. Thankfully, Kane speaks first, changing the subject.

"What time do you need to be at work?"

I glance at the clock on the oven. "As soon as I can. I'm usually there before anyone else."

"And you stay later than everyone else."

It's not a question, but I nod anyway. "Usually."

"You're going to have to cut your hours shorter this week."

"Because we're going to be working on finding Rafe?"

"*I* am going to be working on that."

I cross my arms over my chest. "I'm helping. He's my brother. I know him and his patterns better than anyone."

"Which is why you're going to tell me all of it and let me do my job."

Oh, hell no. "You aren't cutting me out of this. You told me yourself that I'm in danger too if we don't figure this out, so don't expect me to sit on the sidelines."

He opens his mouth.

"And don't you dare tell me it's too dangerous. I'm not going to be on lockdown and shut out of whatever you're doing."

"Get ready for work. We'll discuss it on the way."

"As long as the discussion ends with you agreeing with me, I'm fine with that."

I turn on a heel and head back up the stairs, already thinking of the order in which I'm going to unveil my arguments on the drive to the distillery.

Kane hasn't seen anything yet.

CHAPTER 18

Kane

I THOUGHT TEMPERANCE WAS IMPRESSIVE ON THE drive in, when despite having her eyes covered by the beanie, she laid out a four-pronged argument in favor of her being an integral part of *Operation: Save Rafe's Ass*, as she called it. But it wasn't until I saw her in action at Seven Sinners that I realized how much of a badass she truly is.

The woman is an unstoppable force of nature when she gets rolling.

From a guest chair in her office at Seven Sinners, I follow along as she rips a supplier a new one for missing a delivery date, threatening to sue for breach of contract if they don't have the delivery there within the next twelve hours so they don't slow down production.

That's not the truly impressive part, though. The impressive part came when she got off the phone and I asked, "Were you bluffing about walking on the deal?"

She raises a dark eyebrow, crosses her arms over her chest, and purses her lips. "I never bluff."

"Bullshit."

Her lips ease into a smile. "It's the truth. If he doesn't want to deliver on time without charging a premium, we already have his competitor lined up to fill the gap. Keira and I negotiated the contract last month, and they're ready to deliver on forty-eight hours' notice—without a premium. If the jackass wants to be difficult, we can pivot. It wasn't the plan, but I'm not going to let him think he can hold Seven Sinners hostage. Nothing slows down distilling operations, certainly not arrogant assholes who think they've got us by the balls."

"Is there anything you can't handle?"

Already today, I've listened to her deal with an employee dispute, a customer incident, schedule three consultations for special events, test the receptionist on her tour skills, and that was on top of her fingers flying across the keyboard to answer emails, review contracts, and argue with the lawyer about a negotiation point she wouldn't agree to.

The woman is easily doing three people's jobs instead of one, and I'm beginning to think she isn't totally human.

"You need an assistant. Or three."

She shoots me a wry look. "I *was* the assistant."

"You still need more help."

"Trust me, I know. Keira knows too. She left a note that interviews will be scheduled for next week as soon as I'm finished reviewing this stack of résumés and highlighting the most qualified applicants who don't sound like assholes." She pats a pile of papers on her right, which is next to a stack of contracts she already told me was up next on the to-do list.

"Does it ever slow down?"

"It hasn't yet," she answers with a shake of her head.

I glance at the clock on the wall and realize it's nearing noon, which explains my growling stomach. "Do you ever stop to eat?"

Before she can answer, her phone rings and she grimaces.

She answers with a cheery greeting, but I hear the stressed edge of her tone. She might be good at this job, but she doesn't love it. Right now, she's in *grin and bear it* mode.

"Today? I . . . well, I could probably make that work. What time?" She pauses and glances at me. "Now? I guess I can do that. Meet upstairs in the restaurant? I'll bring my planner. Thanks for calling, Yve."

Temperance hangs up the phone.

"What's that about?"

She picks up a pencil and spins it between her fingertips. "Another possible event."

"Woman, you need to eat."

"I will. Lunch meeting just got scheduled."

"Jesus Christ. It never ends. Who are you meeting? I need background. You're not sitting across the table from anyone I don't okay."

Temperance rolls her eyes. "She's not a threat. She's a friend. A new friend."

"New friend? I don't like it."

"You don't have to like it, but Yve isn't a threat. She owns a couple of shops in the Quarter."

"What kind of shops?"

"Well, lingerie, for one."

"So after work . . . you're planning on shopping."

"You wish," Temperance says as she rises and gathers up her planner and a notepad.

Oh, princess, you have no idea what I wish.

CHAPTER 19

Temperance

A FTER A WARNING FROM KANE NOT TO DISCLOSE anything about his identity, my brother, or our current situation, we head up to the restaurant to meet Yve.

I can feel his gaze on me from his position near the bar as I take a seat at the booth across from her. You'd think after being near him all day, I'd be used to his scrutiny, but it's still unsettling. As are my warring feelings when it comes to him.

Before I knew who Kane was, he fascinated me. Now? My fascination is growing to unhealthy levels.

He's nothing like I expected. I thought he'd sit in the corner of my office and watch the door, like Scar does when he's guarding Keira, but Kane shocked me by *helping*. When I dumped an entire stack of invoices off the edge of my overwhelmed desk, he picked up every single one and reordered them.

It took me a few minutes to process the fact that a man who is probably more accustomed to handling bullets than paperwork was *alphabetizing* my invoices.

It has to be completely beneath him, and yet, he didn't hesitate.

I've been the low woman on the totem pole at Seven Sinners for so long that it's strange to have someone take anything off my plate. And now, instead of looming over me in a semi-public space, he's watching from a nondisruptive distance. Well, nondisruptive to everything but my concentration.

"You're as jumpy as a cat in heat. What's going on?" Yve studies me, seeming to zero in on my every fidgeting gesture.

"Nothing. I'm fine. Drank too much coffee this morning."

"Should probably have some whiskey to help tame that buzz then, yeah?"

"Not for me. I don't drink whiskey, especially during work hours."

"Fair enough, but I'm ordering some. I took the afternoon off. JP is holding down the fort, along with a few new employees, and I'm calling for a ride home."

"Feel free. I'm happy to serve you all the whis-key you could possibly drink." I wave over one of the waitstaff, and Yve orders her whiskey and I order us an appetizer. As soon as the server steps away, I get down to business. "Tell me about this event you want to plan."

On the phone, Yve mentioned setting up a whis-key-tasting night at her boutique as a way to drive people into the new lingerie store.

"I want to call it Frisky Whiskey Night at the Pretty Kitty."

I grin. "That's perfect."

"I thought so. My competition is big into cham-pagne and shopping nights, but that's boring. Whiskey is so much more fun, and I think it would really suit my clientele better."

I flip open my planner. "When are you thinking?"

We discuss a few dates, debate them, and finally settle on a winner. During our conversation, I can't help but look over Yve's shoulder a half dozen times at Kane.

When I shut my notebook and attempt one more surreptitious glance, she shakes her head.

"Really, girl? You aren't subtle at all." She casu-ally glances over her shoulder, and from her shift in posture, I know the moment she spots him. Her attention swings back to me.

"Now I get it. Who's the lucky man?" She pauses, holding up a finger. "Wait. That's him, isn't it? The one you had the thing for that you didn't know his name?"

"Shhh. Please don't say anything. It's not a thing. There's nothing happening. It's no big deal."

She leans back in the booth and tilts her chin. "You're a terrible liar. That's totally him. Now I see why you kept going back. I would've too. You know, if I didn't have my own man. He's delicious."

"It's nothing. Really. It's not going anywhere." Even as I say the words, I want to snatch them back because I don't want them to be true. Then again, how can they be anything but the truth?

He's a hit man. We're going to track down my brother, figure out how to keep him and me safe, and get rid of the people who want him dead. And then . . . it's over. Simple as that.

Yve's gaze turns mocking. "Girl, I know all about not wanting to get involved with a guy. I even know all about hating a guy, or at least telling myself I do, which clearly isn't your issue here. Sometimes the universe has different plans than you do, and there's not a damn thing you can do about it." She pretends to reach for her purse that hangs on the end of our booth and glances over her shoulder again. A moment later, she turns back to me. "He can't take his eyes off you."

"It's not what you think."

"Pshh, girl. He's practically eating you alive. That man looks like he'd drag you into a corner and have his way with you just as soon as eat that burger in front of him."

She isn't lying. When Kane's gaze sweeps over me, there's no denying the hunger.

"I don't know what to do," I whisper.

"Is he a good man?"

Yve's question should be an easy one to answer, but I freeze. *Is Kane a good man?*

"I guess that depends on how you define *good*."

"He hit you? Talk down to you? Make you feel stupid?"

Yve's stare is intense, and I hate to think she has experience with any of those things, but given the sharpness in her tone, I know she must.

"No. Definitely not."

"Is he inconsiderate? A liar? An asshole? Mean to kids and dogs?"

I shake my head. "No. Although I've never seen him with a kid or a dog."

"You think he'd be a dick to them?"

I try to picture it, but I truly can't. "I can't imagine he would be."

"Would he hide a body for you?"

That question takes me completely off guard. "What?"

"Would he cover your ass no matter what? You get that feeling from him?"

She doesn't know it, but he's already committed to physically covering my ass and doing whatever else he can to help me.

"Yes. He would," I reply unequivocally.

"He's kind to you? Helpful? Always make sure you come?"

It's lucky I'm not chewing because I would have choked. "Oh yeah."

"Then he's a good man, or at least a good enough one."

I contemplate her requirements for being a good man, and I'm a little stunned. All the things she said—the positives and the negatives—would separate bad from good . . . but there's so much more to it. Isn't there?

"*No amount of money can make me take a job if I won't be able to live with myself after it's done.*"

That's what Kane said when I dropped the bomb of a question on him this morning.

He might do bad things, but does that make him a bad person? My brother does things that plenty of people would classify as bad, but he loves me like crazy and would do anything for me. I don't think he's a bad person.

At the end of the day, that's what truly matters. *Isn't it?*

Yve's comments leave me with plenty to think about for the rest of the day, made even more complicated by the man across the desk from me.

Kane's presence makes me hyperaware of every movement I make, down to the slide of my blouse across my skin. In the middle of reviewing résumés, my mind wanders to what happened in the shower last night, and the strange mix of vulnerability and strength it revealed.

My concentration completely blown, I slap my laptop closed. "I'm done for the day."

Kane's eyebrows rise. "You sure?"

I nod. "Yep. Hit the wall."

He stands and stretches. "Finally. I pull plenty of long days, but you're a workhorse."

"I'm not sure I like that description."

I unplug my laptop and spin my chair around to grab my bag off the floor to pack it up. Once I have it in my hands, I straighten in my chair, intending to spin back around, but Kane is behind me. I didn't hear him move, but I can feel him there.

"You're smart. Determined. Disciplined. I'm impressed. I meant it as a compliment."

I want to curl up in his heat and his clean, spicy scent, but his kind words make me wary. Like I'm missing something.

I spin around in my chair to face him. "Why do I feel like you want something from me?"

He wraps a hand around each of the arms of my chair, caging me in. "Because I do."

My heart stutters. "What?"

"You, naked."

Heat flares in my belly, not just at his words but from the need rolling off him. I want to bend. Give him everything he wants. And that scares me.

How did I let him gain this much power over me?

"You don't need to soften me up with flattery to get that, as we both know."

I try to look away, but he rolls the chair closer to him and captures my attention once more.

"What the hell does that mean?"

I glare. "I'm already fucking you. There's no need

to turn on the charm now. It's pretty much a fore-gone conclusion . . . unless there's something else you're after."

His gaze narrows, and for long moments, a heavy silence builds between us like crates of dynamite.

"You don't see it. How the fuck do you not see it?" His brows dive together as he shakes his head.

"What are you talking about?"

"You still don't have the first clue about your own self-worth."

I bristle at his comment. "I don't know what you're talking about."

"Obviously." He pushes off the arms of the chair and rises. "Let's go. I'm hungry."

CHAPTER 20

Temperance

THE TENSE MOOD LASTS UNTIL WE'RE BACK AT Kane's place.

How dare he say I don't know my own self-worth? Like he's some kind of authority on me, and I'm clueless? I have no illusions about who and what I am.

When the garage door closes behind us, I yank the beanie off my head. "Are you going to make me wear that every time?"

He grunts.

Oh, great. Now he's not speaking. Excellent.

I'm still collecting my things when he opens the door to let me out of the car we drove today. I didn't see this one in the collection of four-wheel drives, but that's probably because it's not quite as tall and was hidden between them. It's a nondescript black Audi sedan with blacked-out windows that makes me think of the *Transporter*, which is probably appropriate. Although, Kane has Jason Statham beat on every level, including sheer badass-ness.

He takes my bag from off my shoulder and carries it to the elevator, but lets me keep my purse.

"So, what's for dinner?" I ask to break the awkward silence growing in the elevator.

"Gator."

I whip my head around to look at him. "Seriously? Trying to make the swamp girl feel at home?"

His expression darkens. "You need to work on knocking that chip off your shoulder. It's starting to get bigger than your head. Maybe I just like gator. Lean meat. Healthy. And I started it marinating this morning."

"Oh," I whisper.

He doesn't reply, and the elevator clangs into place when it reaches the third floor.

"What's on the second floor?" I ask as he opens the gate.

"Nunya."

I open my mouth to ask *what?* But then it clicks. "None of my business? Like your company name? Very cute, by the way."

His expression finally softens. "I do have a sense of humor."

As we exit the elevator, I'm still holding on to my question like a dog with a bone. "You're really not going to give me a clue? None at all?"

"It's where I work."

"Ah, the heart of the bat cave." This comment at least pries a laugh out of him.

"Something like that."

"Still nothing on my brother?"

Kane shakes his head. "I've got trackers set up to ping if he uses a credit card or surfaces in any other traceable way, including a network of contacts. But Ransom is good at going to ground. Using you is the best leverage they'd have to draw him out."

"But that's not going to happen."

"No. We're not going to let that happen." He turns away and heads for the fridge. "If gator isn't okay with you, I've got chicken."

I take a seat at the bar. "Gator's fine. Tastes like chicken anyway."

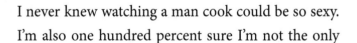

I never knew watching a man cook could be so sexy. I'm also one hundred percent sure I'm not the only woman to have this thought. However, I'm pretty sure I'm the only woman to have this thought with Kane . . . *whatever his last name is.*

I tell myself I don't need to know it, but I'm lying.

I want to know it and every other damn thing about him, which is all wrong. I cut things off at the club when I was starting to get attached because I knew better, but now that things have shifted, it's like my common sense has left the building.

Kane is dangerous, and it doesn't have a damn thing to do with the fact that he could probably skewer me right now with the knife in his hand as he chops veggies. Being in close proximity to him and seeing him as more than a guy who fucks like a god is wearing me down.

Speaking of fucking like a god . . . I remember what he said in my office about wanting me naked, and my nipples peak against my blouse. Why I wore white with a sheer bra when I knew he was going to be around is another fabulous question.

Removing that combination from my wardrobe.

I spin around on the super-cool industrial bar-stool and tear my gaze off the muscles in his arms as he slices and dices, because I can't handle the sexiness.

I pop off my seat, determined to put distance

between us so I can clear my head of all the crazy in it. I stop in front of a shelf that has books stacked haphazardly that somehow manage to look messy-chic. Next to the books is a carved wooden bowl with feet that has smaller wooden bowls resting inside it.

I lift a small one out carefully. "Is this . . . a coconut shell?"

Kane looks over his shoulder, sees where I'm standing, and nods. "It's for kava."

"Kava?"

"It's a drink usually made by island people. I was gifted those bowls by a village elder in Fiji."

From the photographs around his loft, I assumed he was well traveled, but tossing out phrases like *village elder in Fiji* makes me think that his travel is nothing like that of the distillery employees going on their cruises to Mexico out of Port of New Orleans. One more thing I've never done.

"Fiji? Wow."

"I prefer it to Tahiti. Less commercial. Plenty of remote places to get lost. Good people too."

He sounds so sophisticated and I'm . . . not.

"I've never left the state of Louisiana."

This time, he turns to stare at me. "Really?"

I shake my head. "No. We didn't have the money growing up. Vacation as a kid was a day trip to the city. Watching a funeral parade, maybe. In college, I worked anytime I wasn't in class or studying. I didn't have extra cash to go to Panama City or wherever else people went for spring break."

"You'd love Fiji."

"I'm sure." I laugh. "Who wouldn't?"

He smiles. "You'd probably hate kava, though. At least at first. It looks like dirty water and kind of tastes like it too. It's a root that's ground up and put in a bag and soaked."

"Why the hell would anyone want to drink that? It sounds disgusting."

As soon as I say it, I regret it because his smile widens and *he has dimples*. How is this even fair? Oh, right, it's not.

"After a long day of work, the men gather around as one of them makes kava. They sit and drink bowl after bowl of it. After twenty or so, you get a sense of euphoria with some sedative effects. It's relaxing, and some say mildly hallucinogenic."

"Twenty bowls? Of stuff that tastes like dirty water? That sounds like way too much work to get fucked up."

The dimples reappear again, and I'm caring less and less about Fiji and kava.

"That's what they have, and it's an ancient

tradition. It's how they relax and connect. It's part of their heritage."

"And why did the village elder gift this to you?"

"I did him a favor."

"Who did you kill?" The question pops out, and I want to kick myself when his smile disappears.

"No one." Kane drops his gaze and resumes chopping.

I return the small bowl to the set and leave the living room for the kitchen to stand beside him. "That was a dick thing to say. I'm sorry."

His hand stills over the stalk of celery. He lifts his eyes to mine, and they flash with intensity. "There's a whole hell of a lot more to me than what I do. For some reason, I thought you might understand that, but apparently you don't."

"I'm sorry." I suck in a breath and release it. "I . . . I'm not good at this. I don't have friends. I don't have relationships. I have my brother. At least, I did." I shake my head. "I'm not making excuses, I'm just telling you . . . I grew up in a shack on the swamp, taught myself to write the alphabet using a stick and the dirt. When we couldn't afford the gas to get me to school for a couple years, Ma taught me with books that Rafe stole. I'm not normal, Kane. I don't know what normal is."

His features soften and so does the hardness in his eyes. "I don't know what normal is either, so I guess that means we're on the same page."

The knife clatters to the counter and he takes a step toward me, trapping me against the counter.

"Normal's overrated," I whisper.

"Damn right."

Kane tilts his head and skims his lips over mine. "Dinner's gonna be late, because I've been dying to kiss you all damn day. I told myself I'd hold out, but I lied."

His kiss is an enigma, just like the man. Hard and soft at the same time. Complicated yet simple. And most of all—mind-blowingly delicious.

He doesn't just use his lips. He uses his whole body. With his hands buried in my hair, he spins me around and walks me backward until I'm pressed against the lower cabinets on the other side of the kitchen.

When he finally releases my hair, leaving it in a tumbled mess around my shoulders, he pulls back. "I'm gonna fuck you right here unless you say otherwise."

I stay silent. Dinner can wait.

CHAPTER 21

Kane

PUSH AWAY FROM MY DESK AND GLANCE UP AT the clock.

Three a.m.

I've been digging for hours and haven't gotten a single hit on Ransom. I have to get in touch with him or this situation is going to be even more fucked.

When Mount called me in, not only did he not realize I already had a connection to Temperance, he also didn't realize what cargo Ransom hadn't delivered that started this whole situation.

People.

Ransom stepped in the wrong pile of shit. Took a bad job. Why, I don't have a fucking clue, because he's always hated human traffickers.

Now he's hiding out somewhere with human

cargo, because I'm guessing he couldn't live with himself if he finished the job. Even though I want to knock his teeth down his throat for putting his sister in danger, I can't blame him.

I still don't know who was supposed to take delivery of the cargo, but given the disaster on our hands, it's someone who can't afford to get caught, hence the high-paying hit and the urgency.

They wanted the job done in two weeks. I countered with six. We settled on a month, but I got the sense they weren't happy. Which means my exclusivity period might not be worth a shit. If I'm right about how far up this goes, we have a hell of a lot less time before everything goes to shit, and there are more people looking for Ransom right now than just me.

I have to find him first. That's the only option.

"I think I have an idea," Temperance says, her voice startling me as I slide back into bed.

"You should be asleep." In the dark of the room, I can barely make out the stubborn set of her features.

"Did you really think I wouldn't know when you disappear in the middle of the night?"

I let the comment pass. "What's your idea?"

She takes a deep breath, almost as if she's not sure she wants to tell me. "You have to swear to me that you won't tell anyone else. Ever."

That vow is easy to make. "You want a blood oath?"

Now that my eyes are adjusting to the darkness, I can easily see her scrunch her nose. It shouldn't be so cute, but this is Temperance.

"I try to avoid bloodshed, thanks."

"So, what's the idea?"

"There's a place Rafe might've gone. Or if he hasn't gone there, he might still go there."

"Where?"

"It's in the swamp."

"Give me directions."

At this, she laughs. "Even if I could give you directions, you'd never find it."

"Then how the hell do you propose I get there?"

"Not you. *We.*"

I was afraid she was going to say that.

"First thing's first," she says. "We need an airboat, and I have to reschedule my meetings for the day."

CHAPTER 22

Temperance

THE AIRBOAT SKIDS ACROSS THE WATER AS WE round the turn, and a smile breaks over my face. I forgot how much I love this feeling. It's like flying.

"You sure you know where you're going?" Kane yells over the roar of the engine as I slow down enough to make another slight turn before hitting the throttle again.

"No," I tell him as I laugh. "We'll probably get lost and have to hunt gator to survive."

His hand clamps down on my knee as he looks over his shoulder from his seat in front of me. "Tell me you're lying."

"Can't. We're lost until I find the tree I'm looking for."

"A tree? That could've disappeared since you came here last? Jesus, Temperance. Really?"

"Ye of little faith." I crow in victory when I spot it up ahead, about a hundred yards away. It's unmistakable. Years ago, Rafe told me the Indians braided mangroves together to make it into something they could use to find their way. Regardless of whether that's true or not, it helps me remember this particular landmark. "We turn here and head north for a few minutes."

Kane gives me a look of disbelief but doesn't argue. It's a little like the blind leading the blind, but it's the best idea I could come up with to find Rafe. No one knows these swamps like my brother. He's been living off them his whole life—first for game and fish, and then for smuggling.

I know just enough to get us to one of his cabins—or get us lost. It's a fifty-fifty shot.

I make the turn up ahead at a stump that looks familiar. Or, at least, I hope it looks familiar.

A heron swoops down in front of us, snatching a fish from the water before landing on the branch of a dead tree. I spot a gator next to a log and tap on Kane's back to point it out.

"See him? He's a juvenile still. Got a lot of growing to do."

"How do you know?"

Normally, I would have tried to hide my knowledge of all things swamp, but something about Kane makes being back here different.

"We're in my hood." For the first time ever, the fact doesn't make me feel like I'm *less*. It's just a fact. Maybe he's rubbing off on me.

I spot the frame of the shack in the distance. "There. Up ahead. See it?"

Kane's head swivels in the direction I'm pointing as he palms a .45. "Approach slowly."

I let off on the throttle and give the airboat just enough power to coast toward the cabin. It actually surprised me when he didn't argue when I told him I was driving.

"It's not like they won't hear us coming."

The airboat engines are deafeningly loud, hence the reason we're yelling to hear each other through our earmuffs.

"That's not what I'm worried about." He's got the pistol out front, and he's sighted in on the cabin.

"Don't shoot my brother."

"If he shoots first, I make no promises."

Since I know that won't happen, I maneuver the boat until we bump up against the pylons supporting the cabin and cut the engine.

When I lift off my earmuffs, the silence is overwhelming at first. Beyond the rustle of the leaves in the breeze and the sound of birds and the lapping water, there's nothing.

"He's not here." I didn't let myself hope he would be, but that doesn't stop the stab of disappointment.

"Maybe not now, but he might've been."

Kane jumps off the boat and grabs the bowline to tie us up. I do the same with the stern.

"Wait here." Kane treks around the outside of the shack before shoving the door open and ducking inside. A moment later, he yells, "It's clear."

I hop off the boat and head for the door. As soon as I cross the threshold, I know Rafe was here from the scent of his favorite Cajun spice hanging in the air.

"He couldn't have left that long ago."

"And he apparently knew someone would look here." Kane points at the wall.

Four words are scrawled on the wood, but it's nothing anyone but me would be able to read. Rafe's jacked-up shorthand isn't exactly standard.

"What does it say?" Kane asks.

My heart clenches as I interpret it. "Don't look for me."

"Motherfucker."

"Yeah." All the hopeful excitement that fueled me on the trip here drains away. "He doesn't want to be found."

"That's too damn bad." Kane turns and thumps a fist on the door frame. "Fucking Ransom."

I take in the interior of the cabin, almost as if I'm trying to picture what happened in this space. I close my eyes and inhale the scent, imagining Rafe cooking a pot of gator stew on the iron tripod over a small fire.

"He's not starving. He's not hurt. He's just laying low. But what the hell is his plan? He's gotta have a plan." I look to Kane. "He has to know this isn't going to work. He has to know that he's dragged me into this too. Right?"

Kane nods. "And he knows Mount won't let anything happen to you, so he considers you safe."

"So he thinks."

"No. He's right. It's one thing he'd be able to count on."

"With my big idea a bust, now what do we do?"

CHAPTER 23

Kane

TEMPERANCE MAY HAVE ALREADY GIVEN UP ON this part of her plan, but I'm not quite done with my inspection of the cabin. I crouch next to the woodpile and see a scrap of paper. Checking over my shoulder to find her already heading to the door, I snatch it up and glance at it before shoving it in my pocket.

Thank you, Ransom.

I tuck the burner phone I brought with me into the bundle of wood. It has exactly one number on it, so there's no question who I want him to call.

I rise and follow her. "You think you'll be able to get us back to the dock without getting lost?"

"Maybe."

Temperance climbs back onto the airboat, and

just like the first time I saw her take the captain's seat, I'm struck by how damn capable she is.

Other women in my past would have freaked out at the spider she swept off the musty cushion. Temperance calmly points out gators the way other women remark on flowers.

She's truly one of a kind.

"Sorry to waste your time. I thought . . . just maybe . . ."

"Don't apologize. In fact . . ." I pull a small notebook out of my pocket. I never go anywhere without it. "Let's leave him a note. You never know if he'll come back."

"What should we say?"

"Do you know how to write his shorthand language too?"

She nods.

I step closer to her and tear out a page, then offer it to her with a pen. "Tell him you're safe, but you want to talk to him. You need to know he's okay."

She turns to use the side of the boat as a desk, then hands both back to me. I glance down at the paper and find the writing looks like complete gibberish.

"Really?"

She stiffens. "I didn't make it up. I just learned

133

what he taught me."

"I'm not judging. It's handy, being able to write something that's essentially a code no one else can break. I'll be right back."

Her lips press together as I duck back into the cabin, doing one more sweep before I tack the note to the wall with a stray nail.

You better call, motherfucker. If you care about your sister at all . . .

With another silent order, I turn and leave.

CHAPTER 24

Temperance

"TURN RIGHT HERE. IT'S THE SECOND driveway on the right. The mailbox is attached to an exhaust manifold."

Kane raised an eyebrow when I told him there was somewhere else I needed to go after we returned the airboat to the bait shop, but he didn't argue. Maybe it was the tone of my voice when I asked, or maybe it was because I was subconsciously promising sexual favors. Either way, we were on our way to the scrap yard, and at least for a few hours, I could forget how big of a bust my idea to track down my brother was.

"This one?" He slows when Elijah's mailbox comes into view.

I still remember the day we made it, and his dad

backhanded him for using parts he could have sold. His dad died six months later, and not a single funeral-goer cried. Elijah and I come from the same kind of people.

"That's the one."

Before, I would have cringed at the thought of bringing Kane here, but we've already been to one of my brother's cabins in the swamp. He's experienced my airboat-driving skills and doesn't seem to be looking at me any differently, so I'm going to chance it.

I'm willing to chance a whole hell of a lot to get my hands on a welding torch and some metal. Like a junkie rediscovering an addiction, I need my fix.

He drives through the open chain-link gate. "So, this is how you got your start? Welding metal together in a scrap yard?"

As he scans the rows of busted cars, I wonder if he sees them as potential, like me, or garbage, like most everyone else.

"Something like that."

"I've spent a fair bit of time at scrap yards over the years. Can't always find the parts you need to restore something old in a brand-new box."

Something about his comment fills me with the strangest hope. *He sees possibilities.*

"Follow this track around to the metal building. We can park beside it."

He nods, and we slowly roll through the aisles. "Oh, sweet. Did you see that Wagoneer?" Kane brakes. "It's in rough shape, but I bet it has some good parts to bring another one back to life."

"Who restores your vehicles?"

"I do a lot of the work myself. As much as I can, anyway. I don't love rebuilding the engines, so I'll farm that work out sometimes."

"That must've taken *years*."

He shrugs like it's no big deal, but to me, it's a huge deal. "Some I bought restored. Others, I just couldn't walk away from. Like that Wagoneer. That'd be the start of a fun project."

Warmth spreads through me.

"Eli would probably let you poke around, if you asked. He's a shark when it comes to negotiating, though. Especially when he smells money."

"I don't think he's going to smell money." Kane glances down at his grease-stained T-shirt, torn jeans, and motorcycle boots.

When I first saw him in them this morning, I almost had a minor heart attack. He's like a chameleon. But this wasn't some kind of costume, like he was trying to blend into the situation. This is Kane being

Kane. And apparently all he has to do is add grease and ripped denim to have me desperate to tear the clothes off him.

"Even in those, he'll see it."

"I can handle myself," he says, and I have no doubt he can. The man is more capable than anyone I've ever met before. It doesn't matter the setting, he gives off an air of confidence that's sexy as hell.

And if I don't stop thinking in this vein, we're never getting out of this Tahoe.

I reach for the door. "Let's go inside."

"What the fuck, Tempe? You know better than to bring anyone here." Elijah's tone sounds straight pissed off as he tosses the angle grinder on the workbench and stalks toward us. "Who the fuck are you, asshole?"

Kane's jaw tightens, and I suddenly wonder how badly I screwed up by not giving Elijah a heads-up that we were coming, because it looks like I'm about to witness a brawl.

"Don't you fucking talk to her like that." Kane steps in front of me, his hands clenching into fists by his side.

"I'll talk to her however the hell I want. You're in my house, on my property, and I make the rules here."

"I'm sorry, Eli. I wasn't thinking."

Kane shoots a look at me over his shoulder. "Don't apologize to him."

He faces off with Elijah in the center of the large metal building. There are way too many potential weapons within reach, and I'm regretting my impulse to come here.

"You want to come into my house and talk shit? Think you can take me, tough guy?"

"Apologize to the lady." It's an order from Kane.

"I'm not apologizing for shit. She knows better. She doesn't bring anyone here, and if she does, they aren't leaving."

Kane has a gun at Elijah's temple before I even see him pull it. "Is that right?"

"Please, Kane. Don't. He doesn't mean to be a dick. He just can't help it sometimes."

Kane doesn't even look at me. "No one talks to her like that. I don't give a fuck who you are or how many cars you chop. I will bury you in your own backyard, motherfucker."

There's a long moment of silence, and I wonder if Elijah is going to break or if I'm going to have to grab a wrench to swing at both their heads before someone does die.

"Fuck you," Elijah grits out.

Great.

"Stop. Both of you. Please." I look at Elijah. "He's protecting me because Rafe got into some bad shit. Mount's orders. He's not going to say anything to anyone."

"Temperance," Kane starts, but Elijah's eyes widen as he looks from me to Kane.

"You're one of his fucking lackeys, aren't you? Think you're a big shot because your boss owns downtown?"

"I'm nobody's anything, but if you don't apologize to Temperance, then I'll be the guy who gives you a world-class beating as a lesson on how to treat women before I end you."

"Eli, apologize, goddammit!"

Elijah must hear the desperation in my tone, but I have no doubt that Kane will follow through. Elijah may be a hotshot in the bayou, but Kane is in a whole different league.

"Sorry, Tempe. You know I didn't mean it."

"I know." I shift my gaze to Kane. "Please put the gun away. We're all on the same team here."

"You mean *Team: I've Nailed Temperance*?" Elijah

says with a smirk.

Oh my God! How stupid are men sometimes?

Kane pulls back the hammer.

"Kane! Please don't."

"The only reason I'm not pulling this trigger is because she asked me not to. Apologize again and watch your fucking mouth."

Elijah meets my gaze, and there's a small measure of sincerity in it. "I'm sorry, Temperance. Please ask your guard dog not to kill me."

"He's not going to kill you. You don't need killing." I say it with confidence and know I'm speaking the truth. "This isn't his style."

"If he doesn't keep his mouth shut, he might prove you wrong," Kane says as he lowers the gun.

Elijah backs up, readjusting his shirt and taking Kane's measure. "Guess I shouldn't be surprised that Mount sent someone to protect her. Who the fuck are you, anyway?"

"Does it matter?"

Elijah jerks his chin. "Want to make sure she's safe."

I expect Kane to tell him to go fuck himself, but he doesn't.

"They call me Saxon."

If I thought Elijah's eyes widened before, this

time they look like they're about to pop out of his fool head.

"No fucking way," he whispers, looking from me to Kane. "He's a goddamned hit man, Temperance. Not a bodyguard. Jesus Christ."

"I know. It's fine." I step closer to Kane, hoping to present a united front. Almost as if he can't help it, his arm curls around my waist.

"It's not fucking fine. You don't know who he is. They say he's never missed a mark. Always delivers." Elijah shifts uncomfortably, his gaze bouncing between us. "Never not completed a contract, so he gets paid mad money."

Something unsettling takes up residence in my gut at Elijah's fear and awe. I look up at Kane. "Is that true? You've really never not completed a job? So, Rafe . . ."

Elijah stares at where Kane's hand rests on my hip. "Wait, you're telling me this guy took a hit on your brother? And you're . . ." He waves a finger between us. "*Fucking* him? You've gotta be kidding me."

Kane tenses beside me, and I know I have to defuse the situation before it turns explosive.

"I'm not explaining myself to you, Eli."

"Well, you should explain it to someone so they can tell you how fucked up this is."

"End of subject. Unless you've seen Rafe. That would be helpful to know."

Elijah's jaw sets in a stubborn line, and for a moment I think he's not going to reply.

Finally, he shakes his head. "No. I had a job I thought he might want, so I texted him. No answer. Not for over a week. I figured he finally got busted and I just hadn't heard about it. What kind of bad shit he get into, anyway?"

"Long story."

Elijah shrugs. "Figures. Even a Ransom's luck can't last forever."

CHAPTER 25

Kane

THE SON OF A BITCH IS LUCKY I DIDN'T KILL HIM. Temperance was right—he didn't *need* killing, but he's asking for it all the same with every other word out of his mouth. It takes everything I have not to pull the trigger in the next two hours while Temperance works.

It's not until we're carrying Temperance's piece out to the Tahoe that he drops his last bomb.

"I know where I seen you before. The corner café near Tempe's. I should've recognized you."

"You're going to forget you recognize me now if you want to live."

He bristles. "I don't like you."

"And I don't give a fuck whether you like me or not."

"Stop arguing, you two! I swear, you're worse than Eli's junkyard dogs."

"What? Can you blame us? We both want to mark you as our territory," the piece of shit says.

"Watch it," I snap.

"Enough. Thank you for letting me work here today, Eli. Call me if you hear anything about Rafe at all. Anything. Please. You know he's all I've got left."

The fucker gives her a hug and shoots me a smug grin. My fingers itch to shove my .45 in his face again.

As soon as we drive out of the scrap yard and I turn onto the road, I turn to Temperance and deliver a verdict I know she's not going to want to hear.

"You're not coming back here."

"What?" She whips her head to the side to look at me, and the blue bandana she wore to keep her hair tied back on the airboat and while she worked slides down.

"I don't like him."

"Pretty sure the feeling is mutual."

"I don't give a shit about that."

"Then what is it if not a dick-measuring contest?"

"I don't trust him. He chops cars, which means he's got connections and weaknesses. Someone could get to him and turn him. It's too risky."

Temperance turns to me like I've just told her the

guy is a serial killer. "I've known Eli my whole life. He's not going to sell me out."

I slow for a stop sign. "If you believe that, you're more naive than I thought."

She crosses her arms. "And this is why you're a loner."

"It keeps me alive."

"He wouldn't do anything to hurt me." She says it with quiet force and then quickly looks away. There's something more going on here.

"What?"

"He cheated on me . . . but it was because he wanted me to leave the bayou. Didn't want me to stay and live this life, because I wanted out so bad." Temperance pauses. "He let me go, even though he didn't want to."

"That doesn't mean he won't try to drag you back if he gets the chance."

"It's not like that."

"Bullshit, it's not. It'd be like that for any man who let you go. You think he's not dying to have you back, have another shot?"

"So this isn't about my safety. It's because you're jealous."

I open my mouth to say something else, but I snap it shut. I can't say I'm not jealous. I've never been jealous before, so this is my first experience with the emotion.

Either way, it doesn't matter. Only one thing does—keeping Temperance safe.

I stay quiet, but one question eats at me.

Will I be able to let her go?

Maybe Elijah is the better man, because I can't see how that's possible.

CHAPTER 26

Temperance

Kane and I part ways in silence when we return to the warehouse. I'm still raging about the pissing contest he got into with Elijah as I shower, change into another pair of clean ripped jeans, and get sucked into all the emails that piled up while we were out chasing ghosts. I shoot Valentina a note telling her that I have another finished piece.

How dare he tell me I can't go back to the scrap yard? He doesn't get to make that call.

I wolf down food from the fridge when Kane doesn't reappear for hours. I assume he's in the heart of the bat cave, trying to track down Rafe or the people who want him dead.

Rafe is smart, I remind myself. *No one will find him unless he wants them to.*

Except he was stupid enough to get himself into this mess, which makes me want to slap him upside the head.

I hop off the stool I've been on and pace the floor, racking my brain about how the hell to get us out of this clusterfuck, and where I'm going to get more scrap metal and a torch to make more sculptures for Valentina if I can't go to Elijah's. I don't realize I'm stomping loud enough to imitate a herd of elephants until Kane finally appears behind me, scaring the ever-loving hell out of me.

"Don't sneak up on me like that!"

"You still pissed?"

"Yes." I don't even try to lie. I also try not to notice that he showered and changed and smells ridiculously good.

"Come on. We're leaving."

I let go of my anger for a hot second. "Did you find something? A lead?"

He doesn't answer, just heads for the elevator.

"But—"

He opens the gate. "You coming or not?"

Am I going to put my blind trust in a hit man who thinks he can order me around? I spin on my heel and follow him. Apparently, I am.

"Where are we going?" I ask a short while later.

He tugged the beanie off my head when we hit the outskirts of town. It's dark now, and I probably should be wondering if I made a mistake trusting him, but I don't.

"You'll see."

"What does that mean?"

He grunts and takes an unlit road. It's another ten minutes before I realize where we're going and my mouth drops open. "You've got to be kidding me. We can't be here!"

He shoots me a look across the front seat of the Tahoe. "Why not?"

I wave both hands in front of me, gesturing to my makeup-free face, ripped jeans, and T-shirt that's seen many a better day, including when I got it in college.

"I can't be here. They'll throw me out. It has to be a violation of some dress code no one told me about."

The headlights illuminate the wrought-iron gate at the end of the road in front of us, and my brief moment of panic fades into the anger that I was already dying to set free.

"Turn this car around. Right now. I want to go home." I sound like a spoiled little brat, but I don't care. I'm not going to humiliate myself by being paraded through that gorgeous mansion wearing clothes I'd only wear to the scrap yard.

He brakes at the gate and rolls down the window before barking out *Saxon* to the speaker. He closes the window before I hear if there's any response, but the gate swings open and he continues through.

"Don't you dare do this to me. I'm not in the mood, Kane. Or Saxon. Or whoever the hell you are tonight. Take me home."

He glances over at me. "No."

Lord, save me from alpha males who think they can control me.

I lock my arms over my chest again. "I'm not getting out of the car. You can go right ahead and get out, and I'll be waiting for you when you're done."

He says nothing, just puts the Tahoe in park once we reach the valet.

"I'm not doing this." My voice wobbles, and I'd be lying if the heat of my anger hadn't somehow managed to find its way between my legs.

I will never admit it.

When the valet opens the door, Kane gives him a nod and climbs out. I stay in my seat.

It's not like he's going to—

My thoughts are cut off when Kane rounds the hood and yanks open the passenger door. "Seat belt."

"Not going."

"Seat belt," he repeats.

"Fuck. You." I whisper the two words quietly enough that even the valet, who is waiting outside Kane's open door, can't hear them.

"No, princess. Tonight, I'm fucking the sass right out of you."

His hand snakes out, and instead of going for the buckle like I anticipate, he reaches for the top of the belt, near my shoulder, and something flashes in the dome light. The seat belt drops into my lap before being sucked away.

A knife. No way. He didn't.

But while I'm still grappling with the fact that Kane cut my seat belt off, he reaches for me and lifts me out of the car before tossing me over his shoulder.

"Oh, don't you—"

"I'm taking the back entrance," he says to someone I can't see.

"Don't you dare think about taking my back entrance, you ass. I said I wanted to go—"

He laughs, hefting me higher on his shoulder. "You don't know what you need sometimes, princess. But I see it. That heat running in your blood, telling you to push against me. But what you really need is to show me exactly why you kept coming back, even when you told yourself you shouldn't."

I hear a creaking door, and then we're inside and going down some stairs.

"You need someone to channel your energy. Tell you it's okay to want more. To show you how to take more. I'm not your jailer, your assistant, or your fucking bodyguard, Temperance. I'm your man, and it's time to remind you exactly why you want me to be."

His declarations pummel me, and I'm too speechless to contest them because I'm stuck on one big one—*I'm your man.*

Is that what he is? I haven't let myself consider the possibility that there's any chance we can have something outside this crazy situation. It's been tearing me to shreds thinking that once this is over, he'll be gone, and I'll be left with nothing but memories of the one time in my life when I found a man who was my equal.

My man.

A shiver zips down my spine, and it doesn't have anything to do with the fact that we're stepping into a room that is completely foreign to me.

Kane lowers me to my feet and cups both my cheeks in his hands. "That's right, princess. Your man. That's what I am. You get that?" He locks me in place with his intense stare. "I'm gonna need you to tell me you understand and that you want this."

I press my lips together, overwhelmed by the massive wave of emotions rolling through me.

"You with me? If you're not, you say the word and we walk back out that door."

I tear my gaze from his and scan the room. "Where are we?"

"A BDSM room."

A rush of excitement hits me, and my thighs clench together.

"Yes or no, Temperance. Make your decision."

It's already a foregone conclusion what I'm going to say. It always is with Kane.

"Yes."

As soon as the word leaves my lips, Kane releases my face, picks me up, and bends me over some kind of bench.

"What are you doing?"

"Making sure there's no fucking confusion about who you belong to. Have you ever been restrained?" he asks.

"No."

"You're about to be. If it's too much, all you have to do is say no, or stop. You don't need a fancy safe word to get me to quit if you've had enough." He pauses with his hand on my ankle. "You good with that?"

"Yes."

"Good girl." He wraps restraints around my ankles and wrists, then buckles them.

I tug at the softly lined cuffs and my heart beats faster, this time not out of anger, but anticipation mixed with a small dose of fear. His hands wrap around my waist, and I soak in the warmth of his body. This man has unleashed something wild in me. Something that needs his brand of dominance to be satisfied.

Kane makes quick work of the button on my jeans, and he tugs them down over my ass, along with my thong, and wastes no time delivering the first light smack to my right cheek.

My spine arches, as if seeking more.

"You think I don't know you need this? You think I can't tell when you're feeling unsure and scared and don't know how to ask for what you need to make it all go away? I see you, Temperance. I see every single part of you—even the ones you don't want to see yourself."

How does he see that part of me when I'm afraid to admit it exists?

He lands another strike, and I push into it. He

rubs my heated skin, soothing the burn and intensifying it at the same time.

"This ass? It's mine. I will spank it, plug it, fuck it, and do whatever else I want to it." Another blow connects and I moan. "And you're going to love every single goddamn minute of it because . . . *You. Are. Mine.*" He punctuates each blow with another slap, lighting up every nerve ending under my skin.

I'm aching for him. If I weren't strapped down, I'd be climbing him and begging.

"Please—" The word comes out plaintive.

"What, princess? You need more?"

"Yes," I whisper.

"You're gonna get all you can handle. I promise you that." He lands three more blows on my cheeks before tapping my inner thighs.

"Spread your knees. I want to see how wet my pussy is."

His pussy. It shouldn't send a shiver of pleasure through me to hear him declare ownership of my body . . . but it does. This is the man I never thought I'd be able to keep, but it seems he's claimed me—which means I get to claim him. Keep him.

I've never wanted to keep someone like I want to keep Kane.

He reaches between my legs from behind, and

the pads of his fingers slide through my wetness. "Always so fucking wet. So ready for me. You love this, don't you?"

I attempt to hold back another moan, but it escapes as he pushes a thick finger inside me. "Yes."

He fucks me with one finger until I'm nearing the edge of sanity, tugging at my restraints, attempting to free myself from this captivity. But, really, all I want is more of whatever he wants to give me.

And then he drags his soaked finger back from my pussy toward my ass.

"Tell me no if you want me to stop right now and leave this pretty little asshole alone." He circles the tight ring. "Is that what you want, princess? For me to stop?"

I flex my hips, pushing toward his finger, seeking more pressure. But he thwarts me by pulling away and delivering a slap to my hip.

"Answer me, or we stop."

"I don't want to stop."

"Are you sure?"

He steps away from me and I hear him tear something open.

"What are you doing?"

"That's not the question, Temperance. I want to know how far you're willing to go. How much you'll let me give you."

I struggle against my bonds.

"You can't move until I let you out. Now, answer the question or tonight's already over."

"I want it all, dammit!" The words come out like a battle cry before softening. "Everything you have. I want all of you."

He strokes my ass again. "Good. Because that's exactly what I'm going to give you. Every single fucking bit of me. To the depths of my soul. You have me, Temperance. All of me. I'm going to show you."

He drizzles something cold on my ass, and a shiver rips through my limbs.

"It's lube, princess. Don't worry."

Before, that might have scared me, but I trust Kane with my body . . . and more. He smooths the slippery liquid over my back entrance before sliding something slick between the bench and my clit that immediately starts to vibrate.

"You're going to come so hard you forget everything, even your own damn name."

With the toy trapped against me, Kane circles my asshole, increasing the pressure incrementally before retreating. Finally, he pushes his thick fingertip in just far enough to breach the muscle before pulling back.

In short, he's making me crazy.

"More," I beg.

"You'll get what I give you, when I say you're ready for it."

He pushes in more the next time, maybe to the first knuckle, but his finger feels massive. It's the most decadent stretch I've ever felt.

"I've wanted to fuck your ass since the first time you walked into that room with your perfect little skirt suit and blouse. And then when you started squirming on the desk when that Dom told his woman he was going to fuck her ass . . . I thought you were going to come right there."

I couldn't block the memory from my mind, even if I wanted to. I squirm now, remembering just how intense that moment had been.

"He told her she'd been shaking her ass at other people, and he was going to show her who owned it," I recall.

He pushes in deeper with his fingertip, and my nipples spike into hard points as my clit pulses against the vibrations coming from the toy.

"That's how I felt earlier at the scrap yard. Watching you strut around in your ripped jeans and T-shirt, hair all wild with your bandana. He watched you like you were putting on a show for him, and it took everything I had not to come up behind you at that workbench, bend you over it, and show him exactly why he'll never have you again."

I should be seething at the scene he describes. How he wanted to show Elijah that I belong to him. I'm a self-sufficient woman and I may not need a man, but good Lord above, I don't think there's anything wrong with wanting one—or wanting to be manhandled every once in a while.

"What would you have done next?" I ask.

A deep growl fills the room as he pushes deeper into my ass with his finger, and the vibrator pulses at the same slow, steady rate.

"You want me to tell you exactly what I was thinking?"

"Yes," I whisper. "Every dirty word of it."

He bends forward with a groan and nips my ear with his teeth before continuing. "After I ran him off, I would've yanked your jeans over your hips and spanked that sassy ass until it was bright red from my hand and you begged for more."

The slow and steady rhythm of him fucking my ass is driving me wild. I push against it, seeking more, and he obliges.

"Then I would've fucked you over that workbench until you screamed my name loud enough for the world to hear."

His words ignite a fever in me and I buck against the toy, needing more. Wishing it were Kane filling me and touching me at the same time.

"I need more."

His finger buried in my ass, he pauses. "You need my cock filling you, princess. That's what you need."

"Yes!"

He steps away again for another few moments before I hear water running and then another package tearing open. Finally, he turns, and I'm desperate for more.

"I'm going to plug your ass before I fuck you, so you know what it's like to have both holes filled at the same time."

The head of his cock notches against my entrance.

"Yes. *Please*." My begging is getting out of hand, but I don't care. I need *more*.

"Not yet."

I hear the cap of the lube again and feel another drizzle on my asshole. Then he pushes something against my hole, and I tense.

"Relax, princess. It's a little bigger than my finger. You can take it. Ready?"

I nod, but he doesn't move.

"I need to hear it."

"Yes. I'm ready."

My nipples are hard enough to cut glass as the toy breaches my ass and slides inside, unleashing a wave of dark pleasure that feels so wrong, so dirty, and so delicious, all at the same time.

"Fuck, you look so sweet with that plug in your ass." He presses against the base, and I shy away before pressing back harder. "My girl loves having a plug in her ass," he says, and something within me glows at the praise.

Then I feel pressure again—this time, from the head of his cock at my entrance. But where before it felt big, now it feels *massive*.

"It's not going to fit," I whisper, fearing that my body can't take him.

"It's gonna fit. I promise." He pushes in another half inch. "You're so fucking tight, but it fits. You're gonna strangle me with this sweet cunt, princess. Sweetest fucking cunt I've ever buried my dick inside." He slides in the rest of the way and we both moan before going quiet, our lungs heaving.

It's almost too much . . .

And then he starts to move.

"Oh my God!" I yell as my first orgasm detonates.

CHAPTER 27

Kane

TEMPERANCE IS FUCKING INCREDIBLE, AND WHEN she goes wild, I'm afraid I'm going to blow in less than sixty seconds like a sixteen-year-old.

Her inner muscles clamp down on me as she rides out her orgasm, and the plug makes it even tighter than normal.

"Jesus fucking Christ." I fight to resist and just barely hang on. I'm not ready. In no way am I fucking ready to come. I still and focus on the rock wall in front of my face, breathing deeply in the same way I'd steady myself before pulling the trigger.

I reach between her body and the cushion and tug the vibrator free so I can finger her clit myself.

She's drenched.

"More. Please." Her head thrashes from side

to side, and I wish I could see her face. Seeing Temperance on the edge is the most beautiful sight I've ever seen, one I want to experience every night for the rest of my days.

Screw *night*. Afternoon, morning . . . I don't care. I just want her.

"More." She keens again, and I pull back and thrust, finding a steady rhythm that's going to take us both straight to the edge.

I remember one more thing, and reach into the pocket of my jeans to palm the remote and press the button.

Temperance screams as the vibrator in the butt plug flares to life, adding a whole new level of sensation. "I can't. I can't. I can't." She thrashes her head from side to side, and I reach up to bury my fingers in her hair.

"You can. You'll take it all, you understand me? I haven't even taken that tight little ass myself yet. You can take this." I fuck her with sure strokes. "You feel that?"

"Yes!"

"You want me to stop?"

"No!"

"Then you fucking take it all."

"Yes. Kane, please!"

She screams my name and I'm lost. The chain of my control snaps, and I lose it. My cock tunnels in and out of her until she's screaming my name over and over as she comes, clamping around my dick. My orgasm boils up from so deep, I'm afraid I'm going to break when it explodes.

Only my hold on Temperance keeps me standing up as I let go.

CHAPTER 28

Temperance

AFTER KANE CLEANS ME UP, HE UNHOOKS THE bindings and massages my ankles and wrists before he helps me to my feet.

My body is still buzzing from the sensory overload, and it takes a moment before I'm able to focus on my surroundings.

Heavy wooden pieces of kinky furniture are placed about the room. Its medieval-looking rock walls create a true dungeon feel, despite the expensive oriental rug beneath our feet.

An open door to a wooden cupboard catches my attention behind Kane. Inside it are shelves filled with toys and bottles of lube, all in brand-new packaging, like a sex-toy store waiting to be plundered.

A small sink is tucked in next to it, partially

hidden by a Chinese painted screen. Like the rest of the club, it carries an expensive, opulent feel, but this one is uniquely balanced with utility and practicality.

"So, this is the dungeon?" My throat is hoarse from yelling, and my question comes out with a rough edge.

Kane glances around like he's seeing our surroundings for the first time. "It's a private room. The dungeon is an open public space. But the club keeps the BDSM equipment largely down here."

He grabs a sanitizing wipe from the counter by the sink and wipes down the bench I was strapped to.

"And what exactly is that called?"

He shoots me a grin over his shoulder. "A spanking bench." He turns back to finish cleaning it. "I think we need one at the warehouse."

A shot of reality twines with excitement. *He's talking about the future. Our future.*

It's something I've been afraid to think about since the first moment I worried I was getting attached to him, but now I'm starting to feel more comfortable with the idea. I'm not about to start picking out pillows for his couch, but letting myself picture us together a few days from now rather than just hours from now is a big change.

But I'm not going to let myself get too crazy. I still have a brother who's in hiding because he screwed over the wrong people. Maybe it's like an ostrich burying its head in the sand, but I can't think about Rafe every minute of the day, because I feel so damned helpless when I do.

I lean into Kane, and his arm curls tighter around my shoulder.

"You like that idea?"

I recall he's talking about the spanking bench and peek up at him from under my lashes. "I wouldn't say no."

The double whammy of his dimples hits me hard when he smiles. The man is more beautiful than he has a right to be, even if it's in a rough, masculine sort of way that he'd never admit was beauty.

He'd be wrong.

"Now what?"

"Now we go home."

The warm feeling I get from the word *home* lasts approximately ten seconds after we step out of the door of the room and into a wide hallway.

Magnolia rushes toward us. "You aren't leaving

here until you tell me what the fuck is going on. I deserve to know."

Kane stills beside me. "I don't know what you're talking about."

"Where is he? Have you heard anything? I deserve to know."

I glance between the man at my side and the distraught woman in front of me. Her crimson corset is set off with a tiny black leather miniskirt. She's practically vibrating out of her five-inch stilettos.

"Not here, and this is not the time."

"You are not leaving until I have some goddamned answers. No one will tell me anything." She skirts around us and shoves open the door to the room we just vacated. "I'll have the valets slice every one of your tires, so don't even try to walk out on me before I get answers."

Kane's expression, already unreadable, turns to stone. "You don't tell me what I'm going to do."

"You owe me."

Kane's jaw ticks, but he follows her inside the room with me in tow.

"She doesn't know," he says as soon as she shuts the door behind me. "But apparently you don't give a shit, so you're going to force the issue."

My gaze bounces between them like I'm watching

Forrest Gump play Ping-Pong. "Will someone tell me what the hell you're talking about?"

"Your brother," Magnolia says as she crosses her arms over her corset.

I stare at her like I've just learned English as a second language. "Wait. You and my brother . . ."

She lifts her chin. "You think he's too good for me? Because you ain't from blue blood either, last I checked."

"Whoa—" I hold out both my hands, but Kane jumps in.

"Watch how you talk to her. She doesn't mean a goddamned thing other than the fact that she's surprised. Why wouldn't she be? You've done a hell of a job keeping your pursuit quiet."

"Pursuit? You make it sound like he was running from me. No one runs from Magnolia Maison. He should've been thanking his lucky stars that I had a taste for him."

Kane tilts his head to the side. "And now here you are begging for information."

"Because even though I told you I heard he jacked up delivering a load of human cargo, you didn't tell me there was a price on his head, and that *you* took the contract, you motherfucker."

"Wait. *Human cargo?*" I feel like someone

punched me in the gut. "My brother is involved in human trafficking? I think I'm going to be sick." My knees weaken, and I look around for somewhere to sit before I fall to the floor.

Kane wraps an arm around me and guides me to a chair in the corner, but his gaze is trained on Magnolia. "Was that really fucking necessary? Does that make you feel better?"

I look up at him. "Is it true?"

His expression sobers. "It's true. And I'm sure that's why he couldn't finish the job. He couldn't live with himself if he did. Your brother has lines too. We all do."

"I can't believe he would . . ." I don't even want to think about it.

"Believe it, because he did. But now someone has to tell me what the hell is happening. Where did he go? If he ran, I'm going with him." Magnolia sounds like a woman out of her mind with concern. It's all too much to process.

"Can we please go?"

"What? You can't stomach the thought of things your brother does to pay the bills? Feeling a little high-and-mighty since you got that fancy paying job from Ke-Ke?"

I don't know why Magnolia is pissed at me, but

her tone flays me.

Narrowing my gaze, I focus on her. "You don't know shit about how I feel right now. And how could you not tell me you were with Rafe? You draw me in here, telling me half-truths and giving me bullshit warnings. What game are you playing, Magnolia?"

She stiffens. "The only game I've ever cared to win at—life."

"Enough," Kane says. "We're done here. I don't know where he is. If I did, I wouldn't tell you. Not here. Not now. Too many ears. Too many eyes. Besides, I don't fucking trust you any further than I can throw you, Magnolia. So you're gonna have to wait while we sort out this mess."

"You son of a bitch—"

"We're done."

Kane pulls me to my feet and I follow him out of the room, wanting to put as much distance between Magnolia and us as we can before my questions start pouring out.

Instead of getting the hell out as quickly as possible, Kane stops short and I stumble into his back.

"In a hurry to leave, are we?"

It's a voice I can't quite place, but when I peek around Kane's shoulder, I recognize the man. He's the one from the night Magnolia gave me a tour of the common room, and she let his name slip.

Giles.

"Yes, sir. I'm showing them out, as they seem to have misplaced their masks." Magnolia sweeps around me to stand beside Kane.

"Ah, Magnolia, darling. Were you being naughty and playing instead of working?"

The guy's voice makes me want to jump in a hot shower and scrub until my skin turns pink.

"No. I'm enforcing club rules. If you'll excuse us."

Throughout this whole exchange, Kane never moves, but he also never takes his eyes off the man in front of us.

"I don't believe I've met this young man." Giles holds out a hand. "I'm one of the new partners in Haven."

"Excuse me?" Magnolia says, surprise underlying her response.

"As of yesterday. I do believe that makes me your boss now, Magnolia. How lucky for you."

She stiffens and lifts her chin. "Isn't that an interesting development?"

Disdain drips from her words, and I get the feeling that she's a woman who will bow to no man, regardless of the hold he has on her. And she's apparently hooked on my brother. I can't even picture it.

The moment of silence extends awkwardly when Kane doesn't move to shake Giles's outstretched hand.

"We're leaving."

Kane pulls me behind him as we head for the stairs. I crane my neck and look over my shoulder to find both Giles and Magnolia staring after us.

A cold chill rips down my spine. I don't like that man, and I dislike leaving Magnolia with him even more.

Kane doesn't speak again until we're in the Tahoe, roaring down the driveway and heading away from the club. "You okay?"

"I'm fine."

The gates swing open and he floors the SUV, spitting gravel behind us.

"You ever see that guy again, I want you to get as far away from him as you fucking can. Get somewhere safe and call me or text me, and don't stop until I answer. You understand?"

The cold chill from earlier returns.

"Who is he?"

"Lewis Giles. He's a state senator."

That can't be all, not from the way Kane's fists grip the steering wheel, turning his knuckles white.

"And?" I prompt.

"He's a piece of shit."

"The kind who needs killing?" I ask, my tone hesitant.

"Yeah. Definitely."

I swallow. "How do you know him?"

He finally shoots a glance at me. "Past life."

I latch onto that nugget like it's solid gold. I assume something awful would have had to happen to send Kane down his path, and I'm certain I'm right.

"Why is he still alive then?"

Kane brakes and meets my gaze. "Because no one's put a contract out on him. Yet."

CHAPTER 29

Kane

I DON'T KNOW HOW I MISSED THAT GILES JOINED Haven. Probably because I've been too tied up with Temperance to be asking questions of my usual sources of information. One more strike against Magnolia, because she should have told me. And now he owns part of it?

My membership to Haven is *done*.

I can't believe he's fucking back.

I could hate him purely upon association. My former bastard of a stepfather's brother. The DA who helped the judge nail all those poor motherfuckers who rubbed the Giles family the wrong way.

If a contract on him ever goes up, I'll take it in a heartbeat. I don't care that he made sure my mom received the life insurance payout on Giles after I took him out. All I care about is that piece of shit stays far away from her. But I haven't had to intervene there. Giles isn't into middle-aged women. They're far too old for him—at least, according to the rumors.

I looked for evidence. Called in a few favors. Nothing. The man covers his tracks too well. There's not a shred of hard evidence that he's ever done anything wrong in his entire piece-of-shit life.

But he'll fuck up eventually.

I don't like leaving Magnolia with him, but she's fierce and doesn't do a damn thing she doesn't want to do anymore. Not with her best friend married to Mount. She lives under the extended shelter of his protection, just like Temperance does. Even Giles wouldn't dare test Lachlan Mount's authority.

As we approach the outer limits of town, I look down at the beanie between the seats. I hate to ask Temperance to put it on, especially now. But I know, for her own safety, she can't know where we're going.

She reads my mind and grabs it. "It's okay, Kane. I just want to go home."

Home. Hearing her refer to my place with that word soothes my ragged edges in a way I didn't know I needed right now.

"Thank you."

She pulls it on and squeezes my hand. "Don't think this means I won't argue with you about it next time, though."

"I'll count on it."

CHAPTER 30

Kane

JERK AWAKE IN A COLD SWEAT, MY HAND shooting out to grab the gun on my nightstand before I'm even fully conscious of what I'm doing. I blink, letting my eyes adjust to the darkness and the warm body curled against my side.

It was just a dream.

But fuck, it wasn't a good one.

I release the cold metal of the pistol grip and flex my hand before turning on my side to draw Temperance closer. I want to surround her with my strength. Keep her safe. Never let anything touch her.

She thinks she knows how fucked up the world can be, but she has no idea.

I close my eyes and breathe in the scent of her,

mixed with mine, and wish I could have a million more nights just like this, except with no demons chasing either of us.

I know it's a fantasy, but for the rest of tonight, I'll let myself believe it.

CHAPTER 31

Temperance

COMING BACK TO THE DISTILLERY AFTER A DAY away feels even harder than it should. Probably because I have to deal with yet another event and all its details.

We can't hire an event planner fast enough to suit me.

I should have been running through my checklist of last-minute items an hour ago, but I got distracted when Valentina responded to my email, asking how quickly I can deliver my new finished piece. Now all I want to do is get back to the warehouse, hop in the Tahoe, and drive to Noble Art as fast as I can.

"I swear, Keira planned her vacation for this week on purpose. She wasn't thrilled about hosting this speed-dating event after Mount threatened to make anyone who hit on her disappear."

Kane leans against the wall of windows facing the New Orleans skyline as I rush around the tables once more, adjusting the centerpieces. He tried to help, but men and table decorations don't mix.

"I thought you hired him to deal with this nonsense," Odile says as she steps through the entrance to our closed-off section for the event. It's only the second time we've used our new modular wall that looks like shelves in a rackhouse, or at least close enough so that customers can feel like they're getting an authentic experience.

She sets the tray of appetizers on the sideboard and shoots a sharp glance at Kane. "So, what's he doing watching you fuss over it all?"

"Observing a master at work," he replies smoothly.

"More like she forbid you from touching a damn thing because she has to have everything just so." Odile wags a finger at me. "Don't you dare try to rearrange my appetizers. I'll know."

"I don't want to touch your appetizers. I like having all my fingers attached." I waggle my fingers back at her.

She nods and looks at Kane again. "Learn from her. She's a smart one. You get too fresh, I'll let her borrow a knife from my kitchen to skin you."

This time he straightens to his full height. "I'd hand her one myself if she felt like she needed it."

Odile crosses her arms. "You got some kind of weird fetish—"

"Odile, please. Not now."

She harrumphs.

"Besides," I add. "I have my own knife if I need it." I shoot a wink in Kane's direction, but he's not smiling. He looks solemn. Like he really would hand me a knife to cut off his arm before he'd ever hurt me.

A week ago, I might question whether that was true, but now, I have no doubt. Just like he wouldn't hesitate to kill anyone else who hurt me.

My man is fiercely protective.

My man. It still feels strange to call him that, but I'm determined to get used to it.

As soon as Odile disappears to head back to the kitchen for another tray, someone taps on the modular wall.

Both my head and Kane's swivel in that direction.

Jeff Doon. Keira's high-school boyfriend who is the president of the chamber of commerce. As possessive as Mount is, I'm still surprised he let the guy live once he found out who he was.

"Hi, Jeff. You're . . . early!" I try to sound excited

and it must be convincing, because he grins.

"Temperance, it's so good to see you again."

He covers the distance between us quickly and I extend a hand to shake, but he tries to hug me instead. My arm bends awkwardly between us as I try to adjust and end up with my palm pressed against his chest.

My first thought, before the embarrassment kicks in, is probably not the most professional one—his cushiony body is light years away from Kane's hard one. I bounce back from him like his skin burst into flames after he clumsily claps my shoulder, and I can feel Kane's eyes boring into my back.

"Jeff, so nice to see you. I'd love to introduce you to my new assistant." I wave an arm in Kane's direction, and Jeff straightens when he sees him.

"Wow, nice suit you've got there, man. Assistant gig must be a good one."

Even to my untrained eye, Kane's suit looks custom-tailored, so Jeff's comment isn't all that surprising. The pinstripes are set off by the snowy white shirt and pocket square, but no tie.

I've never known a man who wears a pocket square before, and I had no idea it would be so sexy. File that under *Things I learned from my hit-man boyfriend.*

Wait, *is he my boyfriend*? I don't have time to address my own question because Jeff is speaking.

"Temperance, would you like to introduce us?"

"Yes. Of course. So sorry. I was thinking of something else I still need to do." I turn to Kane. "Jeff, this is my new assistant, Ken Sax. Ken, meet Jeff Doon."

When Kane told me his assistant name yesterday on the way to work, I laughed and asked how he'd picked it. "The phone book," he said, and produced what looked like a perfectly legitimate Louisiana driver's license bearing his picture as Ken Sax. When I asked how many other IDs he has, and if any were under the aliases Bruce Wayne or the Dark Knight, he changed the subject.

"Nice to meet you, Ken. You from around here?" Jeff asks, and I interrupt before he can launch into small talk.

"If you don't mind, Jeff, I could use your help in checking the table with the name tags. I know you said there might be a few last-minute changes. Can you handle that?"

"No problem. Anything I can do to make this go smoothly, Temperance." He turns halfway toward the table before he stops. "Actually—there's one change I wanted to mention, and I'm hoping you'll be okay with it."

He sounds hesitant, which immediately puts me on edge.

"What's that?"

"My secretary was supposed to participate but she had a last-minute child-care issue, so we're one woman short. I was hoping you'd agree to step in and fill the spot."

I freeze like a raccoon caught digging in the trash. "Excuse me?"

"Louise couldn't make it, so—"

"I heard that part, but I must have misheard you when you said you wanted me to fill in. I have to run the event. I can't . . . speed date."

Jeff sighs. "No problem. I'll ask Ernie to sit out too. He's been having a tough time in the dating circuit lately, but I guess he'll survive."

I don't know who Ernie is, but I couldn't care less if he ever gets a date.

But Jeff isn't done. "Unless . . . how about you give your assistant a test run and see how he does managing things? Trial by fire. Right, Ken?"

I send a pleading look over my shoulder toward Kane to save me from this disaster, but Odile interrupts as she brings in her last tray.

"Wouldn't kill you to talk to some nice men instead of rotting away in your office for the rest of the modern age. Jeff has a great idea."

"Perfect." Jeff's face lights up. "I'll go ahead and make you a name tag, Temperance, and get rid of Louise's."

Lord, help me.

CHAPTER 32

Kane

DON'T LIKE JEFF DOON, BUT AS FAR AS I KNOW, HE doesn't need killing. That could change at any moment, though.

Doon is harmless but so fucking transparent. I don't know how Temperance doesn't realize that he obviously told poor Louise she wasn't allowed to come, until Doon himself sits down at the last remaining male spot just before the first round of speed dating starts. When he slides into that seat, I swear we could power this entire city off her glare—one Doon completely misses.

Even if she were single, the man wouldn't have a chance. He's attempting to jump from Little League to the majors, and that shit doesn't happen.

I had to google speed dating when Temperance

first told me about this event, because I didn't have a clue what it was. Strangers sit down at tables, and one group moves every five minutes. During the five minutes two people are at the same table, they have the quickest blind date in the history of blind dates.

It wouldn't surprise me if Doon signed up Louise as a fake participant just to leave an empty spot. Most likely, he had to figure Keira was going to be here and Temperance could easily fill in. The fact that he was desperate enough to suggest her brand-new assistant handle things tells me that Doon may have orchestrated this whole event just to have five minutes of uninterrupted time with Temperance.

I'm not faulting the guy's taste—I'd do a hell of a lot more than set up a fake dating event to get some time alone with her.

Unlike her douchebag of a posturing ex, Doon doesn't trip even my first wire for a harsh reaction. He'd need six lifetimes, not five minutes, to get a date with a woman like Temperance. And if I pulled a gun on him like I did the guy at the scrap yard, he'd piss himself, then faint.

I shift, once again making a circuit of the room to pretend like I'm keeping tabs on everything, but I'm really only keeping tabs on Temperance.

Even though I have no concerns about Doon, I'm

not about to leave her without protection.

I'm watching Doon and Temperance so closely, it takes me longer than it should to realize there's another man paying way too much fucking attention to Temperance as she speaks to all these different guys who no doubt want to take her home tonight.

I switch positions so I can watch him watching her. He's at the bar, and he's taken one of the two seats that have a vantage point from the main area of the restaurant into the closed section where the event is happening. Unless my instincts have completely gone to shit, he's been nursing the same glass of whiskey for a while, because he waves off the bartender as she asks him again if he needs anything. Forties. Dark hair going gray at the temples. Narrow shoulders. He pretends to play with his phone, but mostly he watches Temperance.

I'm not in a position where I can get a picture of him to run through facial rec software, so I can't get an ID yet, but I will unless he bolts. There's no way in hell Temperance is walking out of here without me knowing who the hell he is and why he hasn't stopped watching her.

My gut says he's working for the trafficking ring that's after Ransom, but I can't prove it.

The five-minute interval is finally up and the men

are forced to rotate. I do a quick count and wonder how much longer this crazy shit is going to go on.

More than one woman participating in the speed dating has cast a glance my way, but they're looking in the wrong direction. To me, they're all potential threats, and nothing more.

The only woman in this room who matters is the one I can't get enough of—in bed or out.

Ever since Temperance picked up that kava bowl, I've pictured her on the deck of my house in Fiji, overlooking the ocean and the reef, her hair blowing in the breeze before she sinks into the pool to float away the day.

I was shocked she's never left the state of Louisiana, but after her explanation, it makes sense. Wanderlust is a bug I can't shake, and even though I have the warehouse here in New Orleans, I have houses in four other countries, and I like to spend time at each of them every year. I want to be the one to take her to those places. Experience them again for the first time by seeing them through her eyes.

She'd love the waterfall that splashes into the jungle cenote on my property in Mexico. We'd swim naked in the cold, fresh water and eat mangos from the tree in my garden, before shooting the world's best tequila and fucking under the glass ceiling in the bedroom until the stars came out.

She'd stare in wonder at the Alps from the living room of my mountaintop château in Chamonix, France. I can picture her bundled up in a sweater, holding a mug of steaming hot chocolate, sitting in front of the massive stone fireplace.

And Spain . . . I can picture her drunk on incredible wine after we gorge on paella and watch the sun set over the water from my villa.

I want to see her in all those places. Places I've never brought another human being. Places I've never *wanted* to bring another human until now.

Temperance changed that. She's changing me.

But neither of us can change the consequences her brother's actions have unleashed.

CHAPTER 33

Temperance

I f I didn't want to strangle Jeff before, I do now. I can't believe I've had to sit through nearly a dozen speed dates because *he* wanted me as a captive audience for five minutes.

I dodged his requests for a real date during our time, but I know it won't deter him forever. That, I'll need Keira's help with, because she apparently gave him the idea we'd be great together.

A new guy sits down at the table and looks at me with hopeful eyes.

I wish I could just tell him *not gonna happen* and then we could both eat Odile's appetizers for five minutes rather than engage in pointless small talk.

"I've never seen you around any of the chamber events before," he says. "I'd definitely remember you."

"I don't have time to get out to these things very often," I reply with a tight smile. "I work *all* the time."

"I know how that goes. My mom is constantly getting after me about not spending so much time at the office."

"You're close with your mom?" I ask, because *oh Lord, you're a mama's boy* doesn't seem polite.

"I live with her. It's so much easier. That way I don't have to do my own laundry or cook or clean. No one can press my shorts like Mama can."

"Uhhh." I release a sound from my throat that doesn't quite sound like a word, but he keeps going.

"And her chocolate beignets? Like nothing you've ever tasted. You want to come over and meet her? She puts on a great spread for guests. She'd really love having some company this year."

There's a lump in my throat, and I'm ninety-nine percent certain I'm going to choke due to shock. I cough twice.

"You okay?"

I nod and reach for my water. He waits expectantly for me to finish coughing.

The awkward silence grows, and I finally speak to fill it. "What's your name again? I missed it when you sat down." His name tag has a scrawl that looks like it starts with C. *Carl,* maybe?

"Crabs."

This time I do choke. "Excuse me?" I blink back tears from my watering eyes. "Your name is Crabs?"

"Nickname. From college. It stuck. I just go with it."

"That's . . . interesting." I'm not sure what else to say to *Crabs.*

"It was the only time I ever moved out and had to do my own laundry, but totally worth it. Can't exactly bring girls home when Mama is waiting on me with a nightcap. Unless, of course, you know, she's met them during daylight hours and given her approval. She doesn't like loose women."

I glance around the room, almost expecting someone to jump out of the corner and yell, *Surprise! You've been Punk'd!* But this guy isn't joking.

"Interesting," I repeat, for lack of anything else to say to him.

I want, more than anything, to blurt out something like *I like sex clubs,* but that's not something I can say while I'm sitting in my place of work. Or . . . maybe I can and he'll freak out and run home to Mama?

"How do you feel about BDSM?" I ask.

He stiffens and his eyes widen. He looks so

shocked, I'm afraid a few of his remaining strands of hair might fall right out of his head.

"Who told you?"

Oh Jesus fucking Christ. You've got to be kidding me.

"Who told me what?" The question comes naturally, but I regret it immediately.

"That I like to be . . . kept. Locked up." His gaze drops to his lap. "You know, *caged*. Until my Mistress lets me out to play."

The buzzer goes off, and I praise everything that is holy.

He offers a card to me. "Give me a call. I'd love to talk more about our mutual interests."

I smile but can't make myself nod, even for politeness' sake.

Another man sits down across from me and smiles with blinding-white teeth. The kind of teeth you see in toothpaste commercials. They must be veneers. They're just as perfect as his expertly cut blond hair, symmetrical brown eyes, and Windsor-knotted tie.

He offers a hand, and I shake it as he introduces himself. "John Trout. Local cosmetic dentist. I have two golden retrievers. In my free time, I enjoy jogging, history, decaf coffee, and Volvos."

"Nice to meet you, John. Decaf coffee and Volvos . . . quite the rock-star lifestyle you lead."

"I like being up front. If you're looking for drama, unpredictability, and wild times, I'm not your guy."

"Okay."

His gaze drops to my name tag. "Temperance. You sound perfect for me, just based on your name. My therapist would approve. Do you come here often?"

I'm not sure if he's trying to be funny or if he's trying to flirt, but I laugh. "I work here, actually."

His expression falls. "I'm afraid we're ill matched, then. I'm in AA. I can't have a wife who works at a whiskey distillery."

"Wife? Slow down, turbo."

"I don't do turbos. Too risky," John says with a shake of his head. "Even for Volvos, which are generally very safe."

We make the most awkward small talk in the history of small talk until the buzzer sounds again.

He stands. "Before I forget, if you ever quit this sinful business and want to look me up, here's my card. I've included a picture of my penis on the back for compatibility purposes."

My jaw goes slack, and I wait for him to start laughing. He doesn't. Instead, he places the card in my hand and moves on to the next table.

I drop the card on the table with a shudder and it lands wrong side up.

He wasn't joking. I throw up in my mouth a little bit as I swipe the card off the table and shove it in my pocket. I'll have to remember to burn it later.

There are some things you just can't unsee.

"You okay?"

A deep voice comes from across the table, and I look up at a man sliding into the seat.

"Yes, fine. I think. Wow. Speed dating isn't for the faint of heart."

"No kidding. I've already had offers for two blow jobs in the parking lot and to get pegged at the nearest pay-by-the-hour motel."

"Uh, then it sounds like we don't need to talk. Your schedule is full." I'm not sure how I manage to say it with a straight face, but I do.

"The blow jobs I'm down with, but I don't put anything in my ass. She was barking up the wrong tree. I bet that guy who was just here with you would be cool with it." He eyes the dentist. "He gives me the closet kink vibe under all that straight-laced, perfect-teeth bullshit."

I want to tell him about the dick trading card in my pocket, but I can't bring myself to admit it out loud. "You want to just drink whiskey and not talk?"

The man nods at my proposal. "Sure thing. I'm gonna bang the blonde at the end when I leave, anyway. Already fingered her a little under the table, so it wouldn't be fair to lead you on."

I shoot up from my chair. "I need to use the ladies' room. Be right back." *Never*, I add silently.

The only thing I can think of is that I need to wash my hands *right fucking now* before I vomit.

I practically run to the restroom, nearly colliding with a server and a patron on the way.

"Sorry!" I toss the apology over my shoulder but don't stop until I'm inside.

Then I scrub until my hands sting.

"Gross. Gross. Gross."

If this is what dating is like, I'm not interested. Now or ever, and not just because every man pales in comparison to Kane.

I freeze as I reach for a paper towel.

No man can compare to him.

It's not just a physical thing either. It's *everything*. He's different.

He understands me. What I want. What I need. Even the things *I* don't understand. He sees me like no one else has ever seen me before.

And I don't want to let him go.

With that realization sending me reeling, I push open the bathroom door and charge into the alcove—only to run smack into a hard chest.

"Sorry. I wasn't looking—"

"Damn right you weren't, and you're not gonna bolt like that again."

I look up into Kane's eyes. "I'm sorry. It was truly an emergency."

His gaze sharpens. "What happened? Someone say something to you?" His head jerks from side to side like he's sweeping the vicinity for predators.

"No. Just . . . the weirdo who shook my hand after he fingered another woman under the table." Just saying it almost makes me puke for real this time.

"Are you fucking kidding me?"

I shake my head. "I wish I was."

"Who was it?"

"Don't make a scene, please. I'm at work. Also, let's not talk about the guy who gave me a business card with his dick on it."

Kane's nostrils flare as he stares down at me. "Someone gave you a fucking picture of his dick? What the fuck is wrong with these people?"

I open my mouth to reply, but the fire alarm starts blaring.

Fire alarm?

"Fuck," Kane growls. "Don't you leave my side. No matter what."

"But I have to deal with the fire—"

"Not if there's a chance someone's trying to cause chaos and grab you. We need to get you out of here."

"I can't leave right now!"

"You can and you will." Kane wraps an arm around me. "Come on. Let's move. Stick to me like a shadow, got it? If it's that prick I was watching—" He cuts off as Jules, our restaurant manager, rushes up.

"I'm not sure what's going on, but we're going to have to comp all the dinners if we don't want bad reviews."

"It's fine. Just get everyone out." I shift back to Kane. "You really think this is because of me?"

"I'm not taking any chances. Not with you. Not ever."

CHAPTER 34

Kane

"**H**AVE THEM EMAIL ALL THE SECURITY footage to you. I want it."

Temperance relays my order over the phone to her office as we drive back to the warehouse. She put up a fight, but I'm not taking chances.

She's too fucking important.

Temperance Ransom has never been a job. Even if Mount hadn't called me, I'd be exactly where I am right now.

I may not have realized that at first, but it's the truth. I can't stay away from her. Knowing she's potentially in danger drives me out of my fucking mind.

When she ran from the room during the speed

dating, I almost killed the man at her table where he sat. No questions asked. No hesitation.

Turns out, when it comes to Temperance, I don't need a contract to pull the trigger. I'll do it happily for free and feel zero remorse.

The only thing I don't know is what the hell I'm going to do now that the wheels I've set in motion can't be stopped.

She hangs up the phone and tells me, "I'll have it by the time we get home."

"Good." I keep my tone even, but it's not the first time she's called my warehouse *home*. I like it too fucking much.

"Do you really think the guy you saw had something to do with this?"

"Don't know, but it's possible."

As we hauled ass out of the parking lot of the distillery in my Audi, I scanned for vans or SUVs that someone might have parked close to an exit for a kidnapping attempt. God knows, I've done it. One stood out, and I've already committed the license plate to memory. I'll run it as soon as I get back to the bat cave.

See. She's changing me. Changing fucking everything.

I like that too fucking much too.

"So, what next?" she asks.

I glance down at the beanie on her lap.

"Seriously? Still?"

The frustration in her tone eats at me, and I try to explain. "It's not because I don't trust you. It's because—"

I slam on the brakes when a truck runs a red light, and we both jerk against our seat belts. At least, that's what I'm telling myself. Not because I almost said something I shouldn't have.

Once we're on the other side of the intersection, I turn left to circle around again to check for tails.

"Because why?" she asks.

I glance up at the rearview and see the dark sedan two car lengths behind me turns too.

Fuck. I hit the gas and we shoot onto a side street, and I turn several more times in quick succession before we lose him.

Temperance stares out the back window. "We have a tail, don't we?"

"Put it on. Please. I promise it's for your protection and not mine."

She huffs out a breath but does as I ask. "Someday I'm going to get to see this place, right?"

"Yes," I say with absolute certainty. "You definitely will."

"Fine. But then it'll be my turn to take you somewhere, and you're going to have to wear the beanie. For months, maybe."

My chest tightens, and for the first time in years, I feel regret.

CHAPTER 35

Temperance

KANE WOULDN'T LET ME SEE THE SECURITY footage, and when my phone rings the next morning, I'm still arguing with him about it as we climb in today's ride.

My phone rings as I buckle my seat belt. I toss the beanie and dig through my purse.

Keira.

"Hello?"

"Hey, how are things going? I heard there was an incident last night."

I am the shittiest COO in the history of the world because I didn't tell my boss what happened, and she found out from someone else. Awesome.

I attempt to play it cool. "It was pretty minor. I handled it." I cringe at the white lie because I was hustled out of the building. "I didn't want to interrupt your vacation."

"You know anything like that is never a bother. We're heading home right now, and I'll be in the office tomorrow. But . . ." She clears her throat like she's about to say something she really doesn't want to say.

"But what?" I prompt.

"I don't want you to go to the distillery, Temperance."

My mouth dries up like the Sahara Desert, and I try to make sense of the words she's saying. "What do you mean?"

"Lachlan would prefer you don't go to Seven Sinners, so there aren't any other incidents there. Consider this your free pass to work remotely for a while." She tries to make her tone cheery, but all I feel is guilt twisting my stomach into a knot.

I wince before I speak, and Kane tenses. "I'm so sorry, Keira. I truly didn't mean for any of this to happen. It won't happen again."

Another voice joins the call. "You're right, it won't happen again." It's Mount. "Put your phone on speaker. I want Saxon to hear this."

"Yes, sir." I fumble to tap the button on my screen to activate the speaker function. "Go ahead, sir. He can hear you."

I train my gaze on Kane's knees because I'm too embarrassed to look him in the eye during what I'm sure is to be an ass-ripping. Something I'd rather not have an audience for, but I'm not about to risk disobeying my boss's terrifying husband.

"Saxon?"

"I'm here."

"You have a plan?"

"Yes."

"You're going to end this?"

"Yes."

"Good."

The call ends, and I stare down at the words on my phone screen notifying me of that fact.

I tear my gaze away to look at Kane's face. "What does that even mean?"

"It means that Mount's had enough. He's ready for this to be over, and he doesn't want it blowing back on Keira or the distillery."

"So, what do we do?"

"*We* don't do anything. *I* have it handled."

That statement pisses me off. "It's my brother who brought this down on everyone. I'm part of this whether you want me to be or not. And now my boss doesn't even want me at work. Jesus . . . how much more fucked up can this get?"

His gaze sharpens. "Put yourself in Mount's position. Someone brings trouble to your door, threatens your woman and her work, you would do the same damn thing. It isn't personal. Besides, you don't even like your job."

I jerk back in the seat. "What do you mean? I like my job."

"You don't light up the way you do when you're talking about your art. You don't smile in your office the way you do with a welding torch in your hand. You don't laugh in that distillery the way you did when you were digging through a scrap heap and found that riveted sheet metal."

Just like I realized before, Kane sees me. *All* of me.

"Because art is fun. It's not *work*."

"And yet you could be putting all your efforts into doing the thing you love to earn a living, but you're afraid to try."

I bristle. "I am trying. I have a sculpture to deliver to Valentina as soon as the universe stops getting in the way. But let's be real—I have bills to pay. I can't just quit my day job on the off chance that I'll be able to make a living from art. I need a cushion first. A plan. A safety net."

"Life doesn't come with a safety net or a fucking

parachute." He shakes his head. "And it's too fucking short to wait to go after something that makes you happy. We could've been hit by that truck last night—and you might never have gotten the chance."

"So you're the authority on my happiness now? On how I should live my life?" I unbuckle my seat belt and twist to face him.

"Maybe not the authority, but I see it more clearly than you do. Open your eyes, Temperance. See what's right in front of you."

I swallow and take a leap of faith. No safety net. No cushion. No plan. "My eyes are wide open, Kane, and *I see you*."

His entire body tenses. "That's not what I mean."

"Bullshit. I call bullshit. You want me to go after what makes me happy—then that includes you. So, tell me, how is that going to work? Because I don't have a damned clue."

He looks away.

"What? No suggestions on how to live my life now that I want you in it?"

His response is deafening silence. I grab for the door handle blindly, blinking back the tears that spring to my eyes at the sharp stab of pain in the vicinity of my heart.

"Temperance. Wait."

"No, I don't think I will."

I shove open the car door, jump out, and slam it behind me.

It's good to know that not all dreams can come true.

Kane leaves me alone for an hour while I take a page out of Keira's book and pace-stomp back and forth across the third floor of the warehouse.

When he finally shows his face in the kitchen, it's not for the reason I expect.

"I got space. Metal. Tools. Everything you need. Instead of stomping around up here, you might as well pretend I'm a piece of metal and hammer the shit out of it."

"But—"

"Offer's on the table. I got work to do." He turns away and strides toward the elevator.

I bite my lip, wanting to reject his offer, but also desperately needing the outlet he's offered me. "I can't use your expensive parts. I use junk. Scrap metal. Not new stuff."

He pauses. "Use whatever you want. It's yours."

It wasn't how I expected to spend my day, but I can't argue that the twisted knot in the pit of my stomach loosens a few degrees with every hour I spend hammering, cutting, shaping, and welding.

I only pretend one of the pieces of metal is Kane for a few minutes. Mostly.

Stubborn ass.

But I can't lie . . . his wonderland of tools and parts gives me new ideas, because he has more than I've ever had access to at Elijah's. And somehow, while my earbuds were shoved in my ears and I was pretending he didn't exist, two pallets of scrap metal were delivered.

Kane disappeared before I could decide whether or not to thank him.

My brain is working overtime with ideas and designs. I find a notepad shoved between two toolboxes and borrow it to spend a solid hour drawing.

My cell phone doesn't ring. No one calls from the distillery needing my help. It makes me wonder if Keira gave the order for no one to contact me, but I refuse to let myself think about it when I have a pencil or tools in my hand.

My stomach gnaws at my backbone, and I finally

put all the tools away.

When I make it to the kitchen, I find a note on the counter that there's food in the fridge for me.

This could be my life—my dream life. Working on my art all day, and spending all night with a man who understands me on a level no one else has ever approached. The man that I'm . . . falling for.

The man who doesn't have a place for me in his future.

Growing up the way I did, I learned not to want things, because so often they're torn right from your grasp. That's why I built the wall and kept people out.

But Kane demolished it like a wrecking ball. He made me want things.

As I warm up the food he cooked, I realize I should have known better.

I don't get to have a happily-ever-after.

CHAPTER 36

Temperance

FTER RECEIVING AN EMAIL THIS MORNING from Keira to consider myself on vacation until further notice, I do the only thing I can to retain my sanity and shore up my self-worth— especially because Kane never came to bed last night.

I work.

Now I have three more finished pieces—the large skyline that I finished at Elijah's that's in the Tahoe, a fiddle with wire strings that's perfect for a tabletop, and a piece that I know I won't deliver to Valentina.

A small army jeep.

Even though I refused to acknowledge it while the torch was in my hand, I made it for Kane.

As a thank-you.

Maybe as a good-bye.

The thought burns like acid, and I set the jeep on top of a toolbox and grab my notebook.

Maybe if I pretend, I'll be able to convince myself the tears staining the pages are raindrops.

CHAPTER 37

Kane

UNKNOWN NUMBER: *Open the garage.*

I knew he'd come, but I didn't think he'd be early. He didn't even give me twelve hours. *Fucking great.*

KANE: *What's the fucking password.*
UNKNOWN NUMBER: *Open the fucking garage.*

I zoom in on the monitor in front of me with the camera outside my garage door. Facial recognition shows one of Mount's men.

Not good enough.

I tap on the contact and call.

"I don't repeat myself three times for anyone." The deep voice is one I recognize as easily as my own.

"Can't be too careful."

He hangs up, and I squeeze my eyes shut and clench one fist over the other.

I have no other choice.

That doesn't mean I'm ready to do what I have to do. *I should have told her this morning.* But I couldn't face her. I'm a fucking coward.

In the back of my mind, I always knew it was going to come to this, but I've been letting myself believe otherwise. Like hit men ever get to keep the girl in the end.

I flip a switch and all the monitors in my office go black. With the slow stride of a man heading to the gallows, I leave my command center on the second floor.

It's time to go meet the devil himself and assure him the plan we discussed is a go.

I hit the stairwell at a jog, and the sound of ZZ Top blaring through my speakers puts a smile on my face before I remember what's going to go down during this meeting.

Sparks fly as she shears off a piece of metal, and I want to take the angle grinder out of her hands to do it myself, even though I know she's more than capable. But that doesn't mean I don't want to protect her from sparks—and everything else I possibly can.

Fuck you, Ransom. Why'd you take that fucking job? If he were standing in front of me, I'd put my fist through his face.

Then I berate myself. *Why'd you have to fall for her, Kane? You knew better. You knew you'd have to let her go.*

"Temperance," I yell, but she doesn't hear me over rocking out with ZZ Top. I hit the power button for the stereo, and she whips around when things go silent.

"Hey!"

I jerk my head toward the door. "We got company. Take a break. Head upstairs."

She turns off the angle grinder, sets it on the workbench, and shoves her safety glasses up onto her forehead. She won't even look me in the eye.

Yep, I'm doing a bang-up job of making her hate me.

Don't worry, princess. The finale is coming.

"What kind of company?"

I shake my head rather than answer her.

"Is my brother here?"

The trace of excitement in her tone slays me, but

reinforces that I'm doing the right thing. The only thing I can.

"No."

Her expression falls and she props her hands on her hips, finally lifting her dark gaze to my face. "Who, then?"

My phone buzzes again, and I know my time is up.

"Mount," I say as I stride toward the lockbox that controls the overhead door. "Now, get behind that metal wall. I'm not risking you being taken out by someone if they brought a tail."

CHAPTER 38

Temperance

"I'M NOT RISKING YOU BEING TAKEN OUT . . ."

His harsh words scrape me raw. This is what my life has become.

I edge behind the solid steel wall that Kane obviously put here for a purpose. Probably so he could use it for cover if he ever had to shoot at someone driving in through the reinforced garage door that's opening as I hide.

Mount is here.

I should have expected him to come, and I'm not sure why I didn't. Keira said they were coming back, and I should have assumed, as problem number one in the company, Mount would come take care of me.

Take care of me.

My blood turns icy.

Is he going to kill me? Have I become that much of a nuisance that I'm better off dead? Is he going to punish me for the trouble my brother has caused?

My heart slams with terrified beat after beat as the possibilities race through my brain. I immediately try to justify my way out of this.

Keira wouldn't let him. He already said he'd make sure I was safe. If he didn't care if I was dead, he wouldn't have sent Kane to me.

Right?

Unfortunately, I have no idea how to answer that question.

The only thing I know for sure is that Kane won't let him hurt me, no matter what. He may not want me, but he won't let anything happen to me.

I inhale slowly, trying to remain calm, and tell myself this isn't going to turn into a shootout that ends in bloodshed. *Please, God. Don't let that happen.*

Two car doors slam and the overhead door closes as I send up the prayer.

"Where is she?"

"Busy."

"I don't have time to fuck around, Kane. Is she ready?"

"Not yet. I haven't told her."

Told me what? My stomach knots tighter, and I

know whatever it is, it isn't going to be good for me.

"What the fuck are you waiting for?"

"It's not like this is easy."

"Yes, it is. You tell her she's going to her brother. End of story."

The knot in my gut loosens at Mount's words.

I pop out from behind the steel wall, and immediately the barrels of two guns are trained on me.

"Put your fucking guns down." Kane barks the order, holding an arm out and taking two steps to stand between me and what would be the trajectories of the bullets if both men fired.

I tell myself it's only because he feels responsible for me.

"I get to see Rafe?"

That's the only thing that matters now. Part of me had already resigned myself to the fact that I'm never going to see my brother again. That I need to learn how to live with that knowledge. But now, hope bubbles up inside me like water through a fountain.

"When? Where?"

"Temperance," Kane starts, but Mount interrupts him.

"Tonight." He jerks his head at the guy behind him. "Get the bag."

The man nods and pops the trunk before going

around the back of the Maybach to retrieve a duffel.

My mind races with what could be in it. *Money? Information? Guns?*

They come toward Kane and me and hold it out, along with the keys to the Maybach.

What the hell is going on? Kane accepts the bag and keys before tossing another set of keys to the man.

"Didn't have a brand-new Range Rover for you, so I hope you don't mind taking the Tahoe."

Why are they trading cars? I want to ask the question so badly, but something tells me to keep silent.

"As long as I get mine back in one piece."

"Obviously."

Mount's gaze narrows on me. "I hope you're ready."

I have no idea how to answer because I don't know what's happening. So I bullshit instead. "Whatever it takes to make sure Rafe is okay."

Mount's eyebrow inches up almost imperceptibly. "You're a better sister than he deserves." Then he looks to Kane. "The jet will be ready at seven. Don't be late."

Jet? The knot in my stomach is back and has quadrupled in size. *Who the hell is getting on a jet?*

"We'll be there."

Mount nods and heads for the Tahoe, which is parked at the door. His man climbs in the driver's seat and Mount in the passenger side. The windows go black.

Kane crosses to the control box. "Behind the wall," he says, and I slip back before he engages the door opener.

As quickly as he arrived, Mount leaves, although in a completely different vehicle this time.

As soon as the door is closed, I pop out from behind the wall and my questions are rapid-fire. "What's going on? Why is there a jet? Who's leaving? Rafe? Where's he going?"

Kane releases the control box, and his expression is totally blank.

"Kane . . . Please, you have to tell me something."

He stops in front of me. "Rafe's leaving the country—"

I feel like someone grabbed my heart and squeezed. Then he drops the next bomb.

"And so are you."

CHAPTER 39

Kane

ALL THE BLOOD DRAINS FROM TEMPERANCE'S face, and I want to shoot myself for not prepping her when I had the chance. I should have warned her.

That's on me. Because I wasn't ready to let her go.

I should be shot.

I take her in—from the bandana holding her brown hair in a knot on the top of her head, to the old YOU BETTER BELIZE IT T-shirt she stole out of my drawer, to her ripped jeans and battered work boots. This incredible woman put her trust in me, and I have no choice but to let her go.

"What do you mean *so am I*? I'm not leaving. I have a life. I can't—" She chokes on whatever she's going to say next, and I step closer.

"It's the only way, Temperance."

She looks up at me. "The only way? But what if
. . . what if I see Rafe and he leaves? Can't I stay—"

I grip both her shoulders and squeeze, keeping
her gaze on mine. "They will hunt you forever if
they can't find him. You'll never be safe. You both
have to disappear. There's no other choice. No other
way." I squeeze her tighter, wishing I could drag her
against me and wrap my arms around her. "It's the
only way you'll be safe."

Her dark gaze carries intense emotion, and it
stabs me in the gut. "You're sending me away. Just
like he did. Being noble."

That's where she's wrong. There's nothing noble
about this. It's a result of me being backed into a corner and not having another way out.

"It's the only way," I repeat.

Something dawns in her expression, and it looks
a lot like hope. "You can find the bad guys and kill
them all. Or you can come with us. Start over. Be
somebody else."

She doesn't realize that I've already done that before, and a man can only die so many times.

When I open my mouth to respond, she presses
a finger to my lips.

"Don't say no. I refuse to let you say no. I—" She pauses. "Kane, I don't want to live the rest of my life without you."

CHAPTER 40

Temperance

KANE'S JAW CLENCHES LIKE I JUST STABBED HIM through the heart. When he winces and his fingers flex, digging into my shoulders, I can almost feel his agony.

Or maybe I'm telling myself that's what it is because I want so badly for it to be the truth.

"Please don't be noble, Kane. I can't give you up. I won't. Don't ask me to." It's strange how threatening to take something away from someone will cement their attachment to it faster than anything else.

Before Mount came here to deliver the verdict, I was telling myself that if Kane didn't want me, I could let him walk away. Now, I refuse to let anyone steal that chance from us, including Kane himself.

He forces one of his hands to uncurl from around

my shoulder and cups my cheek. "Temperance . . ."

I don't want to hear him say no. It's not a response I'll accept, so I do the only sensible thing—I reach up with both hands and wrap them around his neck so I can drag him down and kiss him.

My lips crash into his, and I plaster my body against him. At first, he doesn't respond, like he's still forcing himself to pull away from me, but I won't let him.

I'm no quitter.

I kiss him harder until his control finally snaps and he devours me like a starving man. Like a man getting his last desperate taste of the one thing he loves.

But that's not going to happen here. I refuse to walk away from Kane.

He pulls back from me just long enough to lift me into his arms and carry me toward the hood of the Maybach.

Under normal circumstances, I'd be freaking out about the possibility of scratching the paint, especially when the car is owned by someone so terrifying. But I don't care.

Right now, nothing matters more than this man and this moment, and I etch every bit of it into my memory as it happens. *Just in case.*

He sets me on my feet before tearing his mouth away from mine. "I need you. Now."

"Yes."

With his stare boring into me, he grips the neck of my shirt and shreds it down the center.

"No matter what happens, Temperance. I will never forget you. You gave me something no one else has ever given me—peace."

The words are probably meant to soothe, but they shred me instead. I don't want to hear *no matter what* unless it's tied to the words *we'll always be together.*

Frantic, I grab for the hem of his shirt and drag it up and over his head. I run my hands over his body—his beautiful, well-honed weapon of a body— and commit it to memory.

Stop thinking like that, Temperance.

Kane's hands go to my jeans and quickly free me from them, and I kick them aside before making short work of his. Right there, in the middle of his garage and in front of the King of New Orleans' car, I drop to my knees and worship him.

He will never forget me. Never.

He bucks against my face, and this time I don't hesitate. I swallow every inch, losing any trace of inhibition. I suck and lick and stroke until his back arches and his balls tighten.

"Not down your throat."

He grunts out the words before hooking his thumbs under my armpits and lifting me off my knees and onto my feet. As soon as I find my footing, his hands wrap around my waist and he lifts me onto the hood. Under my bare ass, the metal is still warm from the heat of the engine.

I drop back onto my elbows and spread my legs. "Make me remember this forever."

Kane's nostrils flare, and with one hand at the base of his cock, he steps between my legs. "You'll still feel me tomorrow."

He pushes in with a single stroke, and it's furious and primal. We're two animals intent on imprinting ourselves on each other in a way that transcends sex.

This is primal. Barbaric. And utterly fucking delicious.

I scream out my orgasm as I come, clamping down on his dick, and he fucks me harder until he yells my name.

CHAPTER 41

Kane

"**A**RE YOU READY?"

Temperance is dressed in Keira's clothes and wearing a red wig that matches her boss's hair. Oversized dark sunglasses obscure most of her face.

I hate seeing her look like someone else. *This isn't how I'll remember her*, I vow. I'll remember her with her back arched as she screamed my name. I'll remember her sound asleep in my bed. I'll remember her laughing and drinking bourbon on my couch. I'll remember her with an angle grinder in her hands.

No matter what, I'll remember her.

"No. Yes. I don't know." Her voice shakes, and I hate the uncertainty in it. She pulls off the sunglasses and turns to me. "Are you sure there's no other way?"

I shake my head. "This is how it has to be."

She inhales a shaky breath. "Then I guess it doesn't matter whether I'm ready or not, because it's happening."

"I'll get the door." I open the back of the Maybach. This is the car that V usually drives Keira in, and while I'm not quite as big as Mount's mountain of a lieutenant, I've chosen a boxier suit and used my skills of disguise to come as close as I can to his look. It's not my first rodeo.

Temperance slides into the back but latches a hand around my wrist before I can close it. "Please find me. Promise me you'll find me."

I can't lie to her. "If there's a way, I'll find it."

She nods. It may not be what she wants to hear, but it's all I can offer.

I close the car door and move to the driver's side, catching my reflection the mirror.

It's showtime.

CHAPTER 42

Temperance

I'VE NEVER THOUGHT ABOUT HOW IT MUST BE FOR those people who have to go into witness protection with no notice. Having to leave your entire life behind with no planning is both terribly difficult and incredibly easy.

I wasn't allowed to call anyone. To tell anyone. To pack hardly anything. One small suitcase, and that's it. But when you're leaving your heart behind, what do clothes matter?

I exhale on a long breath and watch as we pull out of the warehouse for the last time.

No beanie. That's how I know this is for real. Kane doesn't care if I know where the warehouse is because I'm not coming back.

I'm never coming back.

My chest freezes and my stomach tumbles its millionth somersault of the day.

Temperance Ransom, life as you know it is over.

At other times in my life, I would have been thrilled to have someone say that to me. Now, I'm devastated. I'm just starting to figure out who I really am. What I really want. *Who I really want.*

And now it's all being snatched away because my brother did something stupid.

At least we're all going to be safe. I remind myself that it's the only thing that really matters. None of us are going to end up tortured or dead.

I can live with anything . . . if we just get to live.

I lift my gaze and find Kane watching me in the rearview.

"You okay?" he asks.

"Don't ask me that."

His jaw tenses and he rephrases. "You holding it together?"

"Barely."

"You can do this. All you have to do is take one step at a time. I'll be right next to you."

Until I get on a plane and never see you again.

"I can do this." I say it to appease him, and because I need to hear it myself. What choice do I have? None, according to Kane and Mount.

I look down to see the minute hand on Keira's watch moving ever closer to seven o'clock, and wonder if that's how a prisoner on death row feels watching the clock count down to midnight on the day of his execution.

Morbid thoughts.

I push them away.

Kane will find me. He feels this too. He's just being noble. We'll have a future. Somewhere exotic and beautiful. Maybe a beach house in paradise.

In the middle of all the pretty lies I tell myself, I realize I never asked about our destination. It didn't seem important beyond the fact that it wasn't *here.*

"Where are we going? The jet, I mean?"

Kane meets my gaze in the rearview again. "I can't tell you that. I'm sorry."

"But you know?"

He shakes his head. "Safer if I don't know. Safer if no one knows."

"What about a flight plan?"

He tilts his head to the side. "Mount has his ways."

We fall into silence again, and I realize I've completely forgotten to pay attention to where the warehouse is located. Not that it matters anymore, I suppose.

When we arrive at the private airport, I see a few people coming and going, but nothing like the hustle and bustle of the regular airports you see on TV. I've never even been to the New Orleans airport, so TV is all I have to compare it to.

Kane parks the car right up front, rather than in the parking lot.

"Are you allowed to do that?"

He turns and looks over his shoulder. "Everything's allowed when you're Mount. Are you ready to be Keira?"

Again, my answer is clearly *no*, but that's not what Kane wants to hear. "As ready as I'll ever be."

"Good. It's go time. Don't bow to anyone. You're a queen now, princess."

His nickname almost breaks me, but I find my last reserves of strength and force iron into my spine. I don't have any steel left in me today.

Kane exits the Maybach, and a moment later, he opens my door.

I do my best to walk like Keira. It's not hard, especially when you consider how long I've been imitating her confident stride.

I didn't even get to say good-bye.

Pushing the gut-wrenching thought away, I adjust my sunglasses and stay next to Kane as he leads me through the sliding doors of the airport.

The inside is open and airy. Instead of being jammed with people, the lobby is almost empty. A woman waits in a leather side chair, and a man speaks to an employee behind a large wooden desk. Out the big glass windows ahead of me, I see small jets parked on the runway. There's a sleek black one directly out the next set of sliding glass doors with a red carpet leading to the steps.

"Is that it?" I whisper. "The plane?"

Kane nods. "Yes."

"And where's—"

He reaches out to grasp my elbow and gives it a quick squeeze, reminding me not to say Rafe's name. I go quiet and search the lobby for any sign of my brother, all the while feeling like my heart is cracking in my chest.

Then I remember he's going to be dressed like Mount, because we're impersonating them.

Kane squeezes my arm again and silently indicates I need to turn around. I follow the command, and my heart thuds to a screeching halt when I see a man in a three-piece suit walk with a swagger through the sliding glass doors.

I've never seen my brother so dressed up in his life. Or with neatly trimmed facial hair. He almost looks upstanding, which is ironic considering who he's impersonating.

I take a half step toward him, but Kane's fingers clamp down tighter on my arm and I freeze.

As soon as Kane drops his hand from my elbow, he looks at me, his expression stricken. "I'm sorry. This was the only way."

One moment his hand is empty, and the next, he's holding a gun and it's pointed at Rafe.

He pulls the trigger.

Chaos explodes as a deafening shot echoes in the lobby of the airport. Everything goes quiet in my mind when I see Rafe grab his chest, a look of shock on his face.

I can't hear myself screaming.

I can't hear anything.

Another gunshot shatters every dream I had for the future as my brother's body jerks again and he collapses, lifeless, on the carpet.

The Savage Trilogy concludes in *Rogue Royalty*.

ALSO BY MEGHAN MARCH

Take Me Back

Bad Judgment

MOUNT TRILOGY:
Ruthless King
Defiant Queen
Sinful Empire

BENEATH Series:
Beneath This Mask
Beneath This Ink
Beneath These Chains
Beneath These Scars
Beneath These Shadows
Beneath These Lies
Beneath the Truth

FLASH BANG Series:
Flash Bang
Hard Charger

AUTHOR'S NOTE

UNAPOLOGETICALLY SEXY ROMANCE

I'd love to hear from you. Connect with me at:

Website:
www.meghanmarch.com

Facebook:
www.facebook.com/MeghanMarchAuthor

Twitter:
www.twitter.com/meghan_march

Instagram:
www.instagram.com/meghanmarch

ABOUT THE AUTHOR

Meghan March has been known to wear camo face paint and tromp around in the woods wearing mud-covered boots, all while sporting a perfect manicure. She's also impulsive, easily entertained, and absolutely unapologetic about the fact that she loves to read and write smut.

Her past lives include slinging auto parts, selling lingerie, making custom jewelry, and practicing corporate law. Writing books about dirty-talking alpha males and the strong, sassy women who bring them to their knees is by far the most fabulous job she's ever had.

She loves hearing from her readers at
meghanmarchbooks@gmail.com

CPSIA information can be obtained
at www.ICGtesting.com
Printed in the USA
FSHW02n0840250818
51700FS